Polyglot

Stories of the West's wet edge

D0192025

Wendy
Marcus

First edition.

First published in the United States of America by Beth Am Press.

Printed and bound in the United States of America.

© Wendy Marcus, 2009

A number of the stories in this debut collection have appeared elsewhere, in slightly different form.

This is a work of fiction. Names, characters, places and incidents either are the product of the author's imagination or are used fictitiously, and any resemblance to actual persons, living or dead, business establishments, events or locales is entirely coincidental.

ISBN 978-0-615268-04-0

Library of Congress Control Number: 2009900137

Cover and interior design by Robin Asher of Asher Graphic Services

Cover photo by Charles Gay

Beth Am Press
Temple Beth Am
2632 NE 80th Street
Seattle, WA 98115
206/525-0915

To my first storytellers,
Marianne and Stanley Marcus

Polyglot

Contents

Shutterbug

The fuzzy blackness inside the rose puzzled him. Mario came close and peered into the pink flower.

"Dani, bring your camera," he called to his granddaughter. She was out in the garden, at his suggestion, to satisfy an assignment for her high school photography class. The bumblebee, front legs curved over the rose's inner petals, looked like a sated infant against a rounded breast.

Probably crawled in there to keep warm, Mario thought, noticing other mistimed blooms sagging off bare branches and frosty patches of shadowed grass. As Dani made her way over to him, he realized why the bumblebee was not moving. Too late.

"What, Grandpop?"

Less enthusiastic, he pointed to the still insect.

"Oh, so cute," Dani breathed, bringing the camera up in front of her face. Then, "I'm afraid it will fly out and sting me." Mario studied the rose's petals. How tenderly they enfolded the bee.

"It crawled in there to die," he said flatly. Dani lowered her camera.

"Oh, sad." She stared at the flower, as if hoping her grandfather was wrong.

"Not a bad thing — to lie down inside the bosom of some soft, perfumy rose and die," Mario mused. While shielding Dani might be his first impulse, at the age of eighty-five, he figured it made more sense to acknowledge death's intrusion into the garden than to ignore it. He credited his daughter Pamelle for that.

A hospice nurse, Pamelle would come home to share stories and strong cups of coffee with him after completing a deathwatch. He couldn't say he liked hearing all the details, but they did give him comparisons for what his own demise might look like. Pamelle sat and slurped while describing her former hospice patients to him: this one was a master of the short trip, taking just a day to die; that one, after life-support was pulled, hung on tenaciously for a week, becoming more and more distilled. She drank a lot of coffee — no sugar, no milk — and offered scenarios, none of which he found appealing.

"I have no doubt you will die in character, Daddy," Pamelle clucked once. He took no offense, even gave her hand a playful squeeze. To him, her solid body seemed built to absorb the terror and ugliness the uninitiated often associated with death.

In the garden, Dani, unconvinced by her grandfather's somber assessment of the bumblebee, waited for it to move, while sneaking sidelong looks at him.

Mario recoiled inwardly at her wary glances. So like Pamelle's, he thought. Pamelle with her stern pronouncements: Daddy, I need to be a co-signer on your account; Daddy, you can't drive anymore. Dani had started using the same tone of voice: Grandpop, you already told me that story! He felt ganged-up on, the two of them reminding him, shushing him, planning for him. Pamelle and Dani usually let him alone in the garden. It was fenced. He couldn't get away.

A year ago, he had missed a step going down his own front stairs. The house he and Della had shared for forty-two years tilted oddly, and he spilled onto the front walkway. Blood oozed from above his eyebrow where the glasses frame dug into his skin. His left leg pulsed painfully. Scraped by the concrete, the skin on his left cheekbone felt on fire.

Pamelle, who had come over to take him to an optometrist appointment, clumped noisily down the stairs and put a hand under his head. "Daddy, are you okay?"

"That damn knee again," he whispered. It hurt like the dickens.

"You stupid, stubborn old man." He knew she was yelling at him because she was scared. "I will pick you up and, if I have to, stuff you in the car and take you to an orthopedic surgeon myself." He didn't doubt it. Pamelle was a sturdy girl, serious about her Ladies Softball.

How he and Della, small people of Italian stock, had produced such a big girl was a mystery, as was Pamelle coming back after so many years, with a daughter and no word of a father or husband. Della told Mario she had long suspected their daughter was a lesbian. "A bitter pill," he had lamented. "She can change if she wants to." Mario had heaped hateful, hurtful words on Pamelle. When he thought about it now, he wished to God he could take them back. He had been the scared one then. Della had resolutely loved them all, until she'd died four years ago of breast cancer.

Trembling from the fall, a dazed Mario had let Pamelle haul him to his feet. From the ground, he'd fleetingly pictured himself dangling in his grown daughter's arms. He swiped at a warm flow trickling down the side of his face. *Take cover!* The thought of being carried, bloody and agitated, prompted a troubling memory. In such a manner had Mario carried a dying Eddie Herzog sixty years ago.

"War is folly," Mario had muttered, disoriented, vertical once again.

"You are folly," Pamelle shot back.

Mario's surgeon set a date for knee replacement. "You're old but you're in good health," said the smooth-skinned Dr. Nakamura. "Why walk around on a bad knee for five or maybe ten years?" Mario liked dealing with this straight-talking doctor. The door to the doctor's office had barely closed behind them before Pamelle had started in.

"Daddy, you'll come recuperate with us after surgery. The guest bedroom and bathroom are on the same floor. No stairs. A huge garden for you to putter in. Too many things can go wrong living by yourself." She'd stopped and looked at him squarely before uttering the sentence he was expecting, "It's time to sell your house."

Pamelle and Dani called him Bionic Grandpop after the February surgery. The month of March was a blur of pain medication, television, and sessions with the physical therapist. April was spent shuffling down and back Riverside Drive with his walker and lifting Pamelle's weights.

In May, while reading the newspaper in the garden, he became aware of the bumblebees. He watched the slow, ambling way one black-and-yellow bee circled the garden, like it was drunk.

Mario had asked Pamelle to take him to the library, where he read that in spring the queen looks for the perfect place to build a nest for herself and her gang, *Bombus terrestris.* Mario found the Latin name strange. It reminded him of bombing the earth. His regular dreams of the war and of his dead buddies were now augmented with yellow-and-black striped planes.

At his six-month checkup, he and Dr. Nakamura chatted less about knee strengthening exercises and more about D-Day and the sixtieth anniversary goings-on. Mario slapped the June sixth newspaper he'd brought into the examination room with him.

"Fools," Mario rasped, meaning the old men planning to reenact parachute jumps into Normandy. "War is folly."

"That it is," agreed Dr. Nakamura. Mario wondered aloud where Dr. Nakamura's father had been on D-Day.

"Internment camp," the surgeon said, arching an eyebrow. "And you?"

Mario was surprised to find his voice gone. He swallowed several times, cleared his throat.

"Where was I on D-Day?" He sat up straighter, his voice husky. "The 301st Troop Carrier Squadron, 441st Group, 9th Air Force Flying DC-3s. Dropped a lot of young, scared paratroopers over France in the darkness before morning. I still don't know how many of 'em didn't make it, but two of the planes in my squadron never returned." Mario cleared his throat, voice uncontrollably thick. *Damn, like yesterday.* "My best friend and a cousin were killed in the war, a downright waste of unfulfilled lives." With deep deference, Dr. Nakamura eased Mario off the patient bed, reminding him to continue daily exercise.

◇◇◇◇◇◇◇◇◇◇◇◇◇◇◇◇◇◇

Two days went by before Mario remembered the bumblebee in the rose.

Coming into a disheveled morning kitchen, he saw the calendar had been changed. December already — a year since his nasty tumble.

Pamelle was honking out front. Dani, stuffing the last corner of toast in her mouth as she hoisted her backpack, yelled something from the entryway about needing him to model for another photography assignment.

Ten months of living with his daughter and granddaughter had lessened Mario's disaffection for the arrangement. Now, he waited eagerly for late afternoons when Dani, with her giggling, longhaired friends, would burst through the front door.

Mario made his way to the garden. The rose was listing seriously. Its outside petals drooped down so far that the bee looked like it was balancing on the end of a browning, pink tongue. Slightly obscene, he thought, as if the bee was dangling out of the rose's mouth. It reminded Mario of a T-shirt he had seen on his granddaughter: a set of puffy lips with a red tongue arching across her chest. Not a seemly thing for a young lady to wear, in his opinion. If Pamelle's generation protested against modesty, Dani's generation had abandoned it altogether, he thought.

Mario spent the day dozing in front of the television, dreaming of France, of jumping out of planes, and of falling on and smashing his new knee.

The front door whipped open. Dani's books landed like an explosion on the floor of the entryway. Could he have slept that long?

"Let's do it out in the garden," Dani called to Mario. "The rain's stopped and the light's better out there."

While the rest of the country was buried in snow, Vancouver, Washington, the wet edge of the world, was green and soggy. The bloated Columbia River flowed a few blocks south of the house. The Pacific Ocean lay to the west. From the skies came constant rain, twenty-nine days in a row, this time. The record was thirty-three. This Mario remembered because it was set in 1953, the year of Pamelle's birth. The giant baby had turned poor, home-bound Della into a preposterous blimp.

Mario thrust his newspaper at Dani on her way to the backyard. He walked slowly over to the coat closet. The scarf was easy. He turned to look outside. He couldn't see Dani but he could hear the scrape of a patio chair across stone. He didn't like anyone watching him wrestle with his jacket. It took a long time for him to pull on.

From the back door, Mario squinted towards the roses, searching for the right one. No bumblebee. He shuffled closer. The remaining roses were all empty. An unrealistic flutter — might it have revived? — evaporated when, looking down, he saw the thing. He slid his foot over the dead insect.

"Turns out I made a mistake. That bee's flown away." He forced a cheery smile.

"I don't know," Dani said absently, peering toward the disintegrating rose. "Probably a bird saw it as an easy target." She raised her camera at crows in the nearby cedar.

Mario used her inattention to push dirt over the bee with the toe of his shoe. Why such interest in a dead bug? No, not just a bug — once a beautiful, productive life, however brief. He wanted to pay his last respects.

He remembered hearing the rabbi's voice as they shoveled dirt onto Eddie's coffin. "What you are doing is the holiest *mitzvah* in Judaism. You are helping a person who will never be able to tell you thank you."

Wait, it hadn't been a rabbi. He shook his head. It was so easy to confuse things these days. It had been little Hy Korngold, who'd pulled one of those beanies out of a shirt pocket and put it on his head.

"Tell them I'm a rabbi," Hy had said firmly to Mario, his superior.

Inconclusive arrangements had been attempted with someone in the French village. An old man wearing a gray beret waited for them outside the small Jewish cemetery. Two military jeeps and a coffin didn't pull into a sleepy, little French town unnoticed. Doors had opened. People stuck their heads out windows.

Mario could hardly translate fast enough into English what the old French guy was saying.

He, Monsieur Gray Beret, was responsible for keeping an eye on the cemetery. All the village's Jews were gone and probably weren't coming back. What did they want with him and the Jews' cemetery?

Enunciating each word loudly, Mario told him, "We need to bury a Jewish soldier."

"Do you have a rabbi?" the old man shouted. A woman shouldered through the gathering crowd and spoke earnestly to Mario. His vigorous nod sent her running.

"She's going to get a priest," Mario explained to the soldiers in the jeep. That caused Hy to pull out his little hat. "No priest is going to bury Eddie Herzog. Tell them I'm a rabbi."

Mario had felt the situation slipping away from him. The priest strode up, followed by a gaggle of breathless villagers. When the shouting and gesticulating finally settled down, four shovels and a bottle of cognac were produced. Money and cigarettes were exchanged, and Eddie Herzog was put to his final resting place with great ceremony and *bonhomie*, at once a surreal and comforting cessation of war's barbarity. Hy chanted in Hebrew as everyone took turns shoveling dirt over the coffin. The cognac was drained. "*A vôtre santé! L'chaim!* Cheers!"

Returning to the garden from his reverie, Grandpop chuckled. "God, Eddie would have loved it." He cocked his head at Dani and quavered. "*Mademoiselle* from Argentiers, *parlez-vous?* Inky, dinky *parlez-vous?*" He forgot that Dani was taking pictures of him.

"Did I ever tell you about Horizontal Herzog?" he asked, raising his voice. "We called him that because he spent most of the crossing sicker'n a dog, on his bunk. He was from upstate New York. I don't think he'd ever been on a boat."

"Grandpop, come sit over here." Dani shoved a patio chair into wan rays of afternoon light. She escorted him, holding onto the front of his coat as he sunk into the chair. She handed him his newspaper. He remembered his glasses were inside.

"Can't see a damn thing without my glasses, honey."

"The glasses will clutter up your face. Just pretend to read."

"Well, look at this, here's a story about Horizontal Herzog."

Dani snorted, "Oh, Grandpop."

"Herzog finally got his sea legs the day before we pulled into port. When he got off the boat he kissed the ground. A new man! One of the smartest, funniest soldiers I ever had the honor to serve with."

Dani snapped, refocused, buzzed about him in such a way that Mario's thoughts drifted back to the bee he'd buried. "They probably have a nest around here."

Dani was used to his pick-up-where-he-left-off ramblings. "I haven't seen any other bees."

Mario knew from reading the library book that *Bombus terrestris* hibernated over the winter, emerging in spring. He'd like to live long enough to see the next generation served by that hapless bee planted under the rose bush.

◇◇◇◇◇◇◇◇◇◇◇◇◇◇◇◇◇◇◇◇

A few days later, Dani returned from school with a shy smile and an ivory envelope for Mario. The photography students were putting on a winter exhibition and reception. Dani's bumblebee photo graced the invitation cover. Mario adjusted his glasses and read out loud, "Resting Bee by Dani Abruzzi." Maybe he had fooled her.

The afternoon of the reception Mario, in suit and tie, waited for Dani on the couch, thankful that neither she nor Pamelle had been home to listen to his efforts as he dressed and as he attached his military insignia onto his suit's lapel. The arthritis made his fingers nearly useless; his joints were rusted, busted hinges.

Most weeks he tried wearing and sleeping in the same clothes. Pamelle's erratic nursing schedule meant she could never be sure if he was just putting on an outfit or taking it off. At least twice a month she sprung a shower on him, never lowering her eyes as she helped him out of the shower and into a bath towel.

"Grandpop, the reception isn't until seven," Dani exclaimed, coming into the living room.

"I wanted to be ready." In truth, he had forgotten what time it started.

Dani let out a sound like escaping air from a tire, then relented. "I'm supposed to dress up, too." The girl actually got out of her jeans and into a sweet peach-colored dress for the reception. Pamelle drove them to the high school's performing arts center, where Dani shot out of the car. "I'll meet you inside," she called, clomping away unsteadily in rarely worn high heels.

Pamelle linked an arm with Mario and guided him into the arts center foyer, packed with chatting parents and teenagers. Pamelle bumped into people she knew. Mario knew no one and ambled off towards the photo exhibit.

He stood close to the photographs to read the titles. There he was, *Old Man with Memories,* pensive in the late afternoon sun. In another, he held his ribbons and military wings cupped in his hands, a scowl on his face, *War Is Folly*. In a third, he was reading a newspaper with his large magnifying glass, *Failing Eyesight*. In a fourth, he lay on the couch asleep, and on top of his feet perched the cat, also asleep, *Horizontal*. In *Wire Cutters,* Dani had captured him grimacing and clipping his misshapen, thickened toenails. He couldn't imagine he'd given her permission to shoot that.

With each title his unease grew. He thought he had been sitting for portraits. Instead, his beloved granddaughter was exposing his limitations, his failings. He felt tricked. He had put his life in her hands, his soul in her keeping. He didn't want all these people seeing such a puny, pathetic creature. He had been an Air Force Captain.

He clawed at *Horizontal*. Lacking the coordination to yank the photo down, he ripped the cardboard frame and it slanted, partially loosened from the wall.

"Sir, can I help you?" challenged a man with a nametag, Mr. Aaronson.

"I…I wanted to buy that one," Mario said shakily.

"Have a seat." Mr. Aaronson propelled him into a chair. "Who are you here with?" Almost immediately Pamelle was by Mario's side. "What the hell are you doing? Leave her pictures alone."

"That's not really me," Mario whispered. "Young people don't understand."

"You're right," Pamelle hissed into his ear. "She doesn't understand what a bitch it can be to grow old." Pamelle kept him seated with a forceful push on his shoulder. "What she knows is that she had an assignment to portray someone in different ways. She chose you because she thought you would make the best pictures, and because, maybe, she loves you!"

Mario harrumphed, "Some way to show it." He spent the remainder of the reception hunched in the chair, waiting for Pamelle and Dani to take him home, his thoughts dark. His dreams that night were of Eddie and Hy and a knot of beret-wearing Frenchmen chasing him as Dani snapped away.

◇◇◇◇◇◇◇◇◇◇◇◇◇◇◇◇◇◇◇◇◇

January was cold and wet, the sun barely a dent in the darkness. Mario didn't bother turning on lights during the dim, gray days. How right the bees were to crawl into a secret place and wait out the long night, he reflected. Let the young people be the ones to eagerly engage with each season. No sense for him to lean forward throughout winter.

Pamelle told him to quit moping and registered him with the local Senior Day Center. After seeing Mario's officer's wings on his coat lapel, the Access driver saluted each time Grandpop lurched into the overheated bus. That was nice.

Not so nice was the way Dani avoided him, took no more photographs of him. Too bad, her loss, Mario seethed silently, eyeing her over the top of his newspaper.

In March, he came home from the Day Center with a picture he wanted them to see, a Polaroid of himself and his new friend Helen. He looked a little silly, but awfully happy in his plastic green bowler, his arm around her middle. She was a Navy man's widow.

"Happy St. Patrick's Day. Where's your green, lass?" he joked with Dani.

"You have a girlfriend?" Dani held the picture, her eyes bugging out. Mario cringed at the question and the tone — they conveyed the same bewilderment with which he had asked the same question of Pamelle so long ago.

"A Day Center girlfriend," Mario corrected. "My bestest girlfriend is right here." He patted Dani's hand gently. A half-smile played on Pamelle's face as she watched him wooing back his granddaughter. The house seemed to right itself.

One April weekend, Dani came into the kitchen, her eyes wide and sparkly, her body language urgent. "Grandpop," she said in a conspiratorial voice. "Quick, come out to the garden with me."

Mario and Pamelle followed Dani to the back corner of the garden next to the garage. Tiny tufts of pink insulation lay on the ground as if salted from a large shaker. A black-and-yellow bee veered away from them. Another bee crawled into view.

"I found their nest," Dani said, excited. "It's in the garage wall."

Pamelle crossed her arms. "Huh. Adaptive little buggers."

Silently, they watched the bees until Dani got bored. "I'm going back inside." Pamelle turned to go. "Coming in Dad?"

Mario shook his head. An admission, of sorts, was taking shape in his mind. He heard the back door to the house close. He was not really following the bees any more. He was as if outside of his body, seeing himself looking a little mystified, even deeply moved, at the way his daughter had raised her clear-eyed daughter to forgive. "Dani," he practiced. "We're like every goddam thing that crawls on the earth or flies in the sky--struggling. None of us intends to let go."

From the kitchen window, Dani noticed her grandfather's lips moving. "Oh Mom, now he's talking to the bees."

Pamelle came over to view the scene. "Nice light out there," she hinted broadly.

Mario turned around at the approaching footsteps. He was eager to tell Dani how the world worked, but he couldn't speak. At the sight of her camera, he forgot every word.

Percussionist in the Kitchen

My mother is on the phone with my older brother Aaron. "You're playing weddings now?" she asks sharply. "My innovator son is banging on a kit for a bunch of drunken Hassids?" I glance up from my history book. Daddy folds the newspaper.

"Oh, my God." She has our full attention now. "They're trying to set you up with a Lubavitcher girl?"

"Who is?" Greek-chorus, my father and I.

"She recognized you from *Rolling Stone?*" asks my mother, sarcastic.

"She reads *Rolling Stone?*" my father and I say as one, rising out of our seats. Enough of this question and no-answer session.

"Let me talk to him." I take the phone.

"Aaron, you are full of surprises."

He jumps in.

"Hey, Charla. I'm playing with the top Orthodox players. These guys were rockers before they became religious. They're stars. They're great. You'll see for yourself when I come out. We're doing a wedding for some big shot in the Lubavitcher community. And, we're getting two thousand apiece."

"Is this a gig or a life-style choice?" It feels good to get a laugh out of him, though he doesn't answer my question. "Who's the girl?"

"It's not that serious, well, maybe it is. Tzippy's smart and has a foot in both worlds."

"Is she coming to Seattle with you?'

"No, no, it doesn't work like that. So, come, watch. It'll be a real scene."

"What should we wear?"

"Dress modestly. Tell Mom to wear a wig," he teases.

◇◇◇◇◇◇◇◇◇◇◇◇◇◇◇◇◇◇◇◇◇◇

Aaron was famous for about a year. Critic after critic claimed to know the source of his genius. Articles in *Downbeat* and *Jazz Musician* listed mentor this and mentor that, while my mother waited in vain for Aaron to give her proper credit.

It was she who had put out pots and pans for her first-born, her prince, to bang on. When I was in grade school, Mommy packed the entire backyard with old cardboard boxes and then gave Aaron and me different sized PVC pipes. I tired of whacking away at the boxes after a short time. Aaron stayed outside until it was too dark to see.

At the dinner table Mommy often filled her best crystal with varying levels of water. Steadying Aaron's grubby hands with hers, she lightly guided his fingers around the edges of the glasses. Later, hands in sink, she inclined her head and listened to him with a faraway smile, the humming sounds from the glasses delighting her as much as they did him.

"Aaron likes it best right in the middle of the kitchen," Mommy always noted with a pleased laugh, stepping around cymbals and bolts on the floor as Aaron constructed yet another drum kit.

Likes it best near you, I thought. It was why I did homework on the dining room table even though I had my own spacious room upstairs. Mommy was always clanging pots and pans, pulling something out of the oven, slamming the oven door. Or, she would launch into funny diatribes about her refrigerator as an archeological site and throw out "ancient foods," relishing the crash of empty glass bottles she tossed into the recycling bin.

The dining room and kitchen served as a homework club. Aaron brought his high school band mates home. They spread themselves and their backpacks throughout the dining room. They scarfed up everything my mother baked and, seeking other distractions before hunkering down over their books, started rhythm drills. First with pencils, then hands, finally feet, until they got me to stomp upstairs. Mommy would fetch me back down, reminding the boys that not everyone shared their percussive pleasures. When she thought I wasn't looking though, she flashed them a secret smile that said prigs such as Charla were not the norm in our house. They all said our mother was cool. She was. You longed to be pulled into her orbit, were grateful when her excitable mass overtook and embraced your vapid world.

The more *Oma*, my German grandmother, complained that my mother was raising wild animals, the more my mother encouraged us kids to sing with abandon, plink glasses with our forks and knives, bang on the table with our fists. She was a free-spirited teacher who stuck out her tongue at an older generation instead of biting it. Oma, my mother's mother, spent fifteen years in Germany before escaping to America. Oma worshiped decorum and ridiculed religion and constantly told us so through pursed lips. "Ever seen an anus," Aaron once asked me. "No," I said, shocked. "Looks just like Oma's mouth," he cracked. Disgusted, I giggled anyway.

Mommy took us to second-hand stores, reaching into jumbled shelves to test the sonority of pitchers, racks and tins. One time, Aaron, home from college, showed me some stemware a pawnbroker told him had been melted down from guns. I wouldn't touch those dull gray cups. Months later, he played me a rough mix of exotic plinking sounds from an upcoming CD.

"That's those gunmetal cups," Aaron said.

"Swords into plowshares into percussion," my father, the professor, approved. Reviewers raved about Aaron's original ear.

Aaron left college and started touring. He made his home in New York City and we didn't see much of him. Mommy sighed when he called to say he wouldn't be making it back for Passover or even the High Holidays. My father would clear his throat. "And who got him started on this path? This hunting for sound?"

When I graduated high school, I didn't even want to change zip codes and enrolled in the local community college. Those coy parents of mine talked about how much money we were all saving having me live at home. Really, they liked bumping into me, and, being the doted-on baby, I knew I had a good thing going at home.

In November of my freshman year in college, Aaron made the cover of *Rolling Stone* magazine. My mother ran down to the magazine stand at the mall and bought every copy. She was on the phone for days.

I studied the photo of my hunky drummer brother. He held black drumsticks across his buff, bare chest. His abdominal muscles amazed me. His biceps were the size of bowling balls. When had this happened? Luscious black curls came down to his shoulders, offsetting those gorgeous eyelashes all the relatives said should rightfully have gone to me. I could have done without his sleazy smile. My girlfriends all told me the "come hither" grin made them shiver in the most private of places.

Brushing aside magnets and notices, Mommy taped the cover onto the refrigerator.

"Oma is going to have something to say about that," I warned.

"It's her famous grandson, which makes her a famous grandmother. End of discussion."

Three months after Aaron's phone call, on a cool Northwest Sunday in June, my parents and I drive to a hotel in downtown Seattle. Below the hotel, white trails of spume flow behind ferries coming and going across Elliott Bay. The blue-gray hulks of the Olympic Mountains stop any thoughts of what lies beyond them. Everything is in its place in this place.

After the wedding gig, Aaron plans to stay for a few days. Still, we're eager to catch a glimpse of him now. The fountains and towering plants in the hotel lobby give the three of us plenty of discreet viewpoints from which to watch hundreds of bustling black hats and wigged, long-sleeved wives with baby strollers.

We can hear the band doing a sound check in the ballroom. Smiling hotel employees swing the doors open. What starts as a rush into the ballroom turns into a riptide, as the band lets loose with a blast that halts the advance guard while the guests at the rear are still pushing forward.

We don't understand the panic created by the guests practically being forced into dancing the *lambada* with each other. Hassidim are supposed to touch only their parents, spouses and kids, we learn later. It takes several minutes for everyone to extricate themselves, right the baby strollers and warily step into the ballroom. My parents and I hang back, just inside the ballroom doors.

My mother makes a sound like a balloon deflating when she sees Aaron on the stage. He has a thick beard. We have never seen him like that. Tiny black bedsprings ping out from all over his face. Like the rest of the New York musicians, he wears a black Fedora.

The keyboard player, the bassist, and the electric guitarist have scraggly gray beards and ponytails and look like they have ridden to the gig on Harleys. The guitar player has stabbed an unlit cigarette onto the end of a string at the top of the fingerboard. A colorful Afghani *kippah* perches doubtfully on the clarinet player's curly blonde hair. Self-conscious until he puts the clarinet in his mouth, he plays with the temerity of a convert.

A thicket of microphones surrounds Aaron's drums. The lead singer roars something in Yiddish and the band launches into a piercing set of horas. Young people run for the dance floor, lunging around the white screens lined up across its middle. Women on one side. Men on the other.

I watch several parents rip tissues into little pieces and stuff them into their ears and the ears of their small children. Babies howl. The lead singer barely can be heard announcing, "*Barucheem habayim*, Blessings to the new Mr. and Mrs. Slesnick."

My parents and I shrink against the ballroom doors as guests carry two tables and two chairs onto the dance floor. The wedding couple is seated and carried off to separate sides where they are raised high into the air to approving cheers. Women sedately dance around the bride. The men, hands on shoulders, fling sweat from their faces like human sprinklers.

My mother gasps as the bridegroom and another man jump onto a table and are hoisted into the air by a swirling battalion of men. The ladies grab cloth napkins off the dinner tables and tie them together to make a giant jump rope. The bride lifts her dress an inch and jumps. To my way of thinking, it is a wedding reception gone mad, and getting louder and louder.

My father shakes his head. "This is nuts."

A grim-faced hotel manager hurries up to a waiter near us.

"I'm getting complaints from everybody," I overhear him say. "The band has to turn down."

"Who's going to tell them? I don't think they speak English," the waiter says.

I surprise myself. "My brother's on the bandstand. I could tell him." The hotel manager looks ready to cry with relief.

I fight my way to the side of the stage and wave importantly at Aaron. His white shirt is sticking to his sweaty chest. He nods and smiles when he sees me.

"Aaron, it's too loud," I yell.

"They like it like this," he yells back.

"Maybe in New York, not here," I scream.

He lifts one eyebrow. "Are you paying for the band?"

A knot of black hats with gray beards comes to talk with the gray beards on stage. "We respectfully demand that you turn the music down. It is hurting people's ears," shouts one.

The guitarist points to the young men lock-stepping out on the dance floor.

"You should be out there," he shrieks, and the knot scatters.

Soon the hotel manager walks in front of the band holding a sign, "The management requests a lower volume."

Aaron yells after him, "*Gey kakn afn yam.*" Go shit in the sea.

I am floored. Aaron has never spoken Yiddish at home. I have been the one to coax a few choice proverbs out of Oma's reluctant past.

The guitarist turns up his amp and waggles his tongue at me.

"Hey, she's my sister," Aaron mock-scolds him.

Another black hat approaches the stage.

"I want to dance with my daughter. Play me a waltz," thunders the father of the bride.

The biker guitarist jerks his cord out of the amp and slouches off the stage. With a disgusted look, the biker bassist follows, towel pressed to his dripping face. People who have been bellowing cover their mouths self-consciously as the last parts of sentences are heard all over the ballroom.

Aaron looks uncertain for a moment and then hits his sticks together, 1,2,3, 1,2,3, for the remaining musicians. The bride's father protectively wraps a black sleeve across his daughter's small back. Would Aaron have walked off the stage too if not for my parents and me?

My father waves me out to the lobby.

"Let's go. Aaron can call us when he's done." He puts his arm around my mother's shoulder. "Aaron went hunting for sound and found one loud crowd," Daddy says, the angry jut of his chin belying his bemused tone. He is embarrassed for my mother. She shakes off his arm.

"It's not about the decibel level," Mommy snaps. "I gave him all that freedom, and he chooses the most restrictive community I know."

I hear Oma's voice coming out of my mother, though Oma would have pointed out tartly the connection between my mother's disillusionment and the permissive way she raised us. Good thing we hadn't yet told Oma that Aaron was in town.

My mother says nothing else the whole way home. Something is making her blink her eyes fast. I have no words to make her, or me, feel better. It is the first time I have seen my brother fall from favor. I would have expected to feel a little smug. All I feel is confused. After driving a few miles in oppressive silence, my father turns on his favorite classical station.

Once home, my mother goes straight upstairs. I look at my father, who shrugs at me, raising his open hands in a classic gesture of futility.

"It's not what she had hoped for him," he says. "The beard, the clothes, the ultra-Orthodox lifestyle. She sees it as a cookie-cutter world, and, if he is really *frum*, he won't even eat in our house." Daddy sits down with the newspaper next to the phone. I fall asleep reading in bed, waiting for Aaron to get home.

◇◇◇◇◇◇◇◇◇◇◇◇◇◇◇◇◇◇

Monday morning I tiptoe through a sleeping house on my way downstairs. I need to leave very early to make my first class. I peek into Aaron's room, relieved to see a familiar shape under the comforter. His clothes are folded neatly over a chair. It is strange to see his black Fedora and a prayer book on the bed table, below posters of famous drummers. A small *kippah* is clipped to his hair. My parents' door is closed.

I flip on the kitchen light and pour cold cereal into a bowl. When I turn around to get milk out of the refrigerator, I notice right away. The *Rolling Stone* cover of Aaron is gone.

I keep glancing at the white space and back at the cereal box, which in my drowsy, and now irritated, state, I think should say *Vex* instead of *Chex*. I want to bang the cabinet doors. I want to smash a few plates and glasses in the sink and wake up my mother and brother.

Mommy, he's doing what he likes.

Aaron, she doesn't understand who you've become.

Instead, I sling my backpack over my shoulder and gently let the front door click, knowing that I will spend the day wondering which of my heart's rivals pulled the picture.

Polyglot

Vests and loose sweaters could no longer camouflage my swelling belly. I decided to say something to my class via our vocabulary words for the day.

Baby, to baby, babies, babied, I wrote on the blackboard, and for laughs, *bun in the oven.* The Ethiopian boys in the back rose up in their oversized ski parkas, and traded naughty comments amongst themselves. I could tell by their quiet, throaty snorts. The Mexicans nodded solemnly. The Russian ladies smiled and jabbered, the Jewish ones wishing me *Mazel Tov,* the others, *Pozdrazlayu.*

The Russian ladies, my largest ethnic group, sat in front, their hair dyed tomato red, shy cherry, starburst orange, cerise, copper, rosy apple, like rows of paint-store swatches. Today, twins Fanya, tricycle red, and Manya, candied apple, were commenting in Russian on my figure and the circles under my eyes. Why doesn't her husband make enough so she doesn't have to work? I found it endearing and irritating. It reminded me of my mother's and sister's caustic gossip. The Russians must have known I understood their asides. Though my English is first-rate, you can't hide an accent. I was far less removed from them than they knew.

Now they whispered, "*Ya tebea uzhe skazala,* I told you so," to my announcement.

"When baby come?" asked Lina, the sweetest, though not the brightest, of the bunch. Dear and rumpled, Lina was always huffing in at the last minute, a button or two missing or fastened wrong, her homework in equal disarray. She was a year younger than I, part of a throng of parents, aunts, uncles, cousins, and sisters from Moscow. I had developed something with her that came as close to a friendship as I had had with any woman in America. Lina sat in the same row as her sister, Marina, and mother, Nina. Behind her were her cousin Masha and Masha's mother, Natasha — no joke. My husband referred to them as my rhyming Russians.

I heard, in Lina's question, concern about me seeing them through to graduation. "Don't worry," I soothed, "I'm due in April. After it's born I'll wear a front pack and bring the baby to class with me."

"Mozer and fazer iz happy?" asked Lina, her cheeks dimpling with delight.

I hesitated long enough to completely silence the room.

"My mother and father are not living," I said evenly, though that wasn't exactly true. But, how could you call what they were doing "living" — stuck in some Russian enclave, in some crummy apartment complex, in some Israeli suburb, ringed by acres and acres of orange orchards.

I had grown weary of their whiny letters about Russian musicians on every street corner and couldn't I find some way to bring them to America? I hadn't communicated with them in many months.

There was a sussing sound of breaths in and out and a sibilance, a sorrowful whispering of the Russian word, *sirota*, orphan.

"So sorry," Lina blushed, obviously embarrassed.

We shouldered through the rest of the lesson, my spirits buoying back up only when, at the end of class, amid the scuffling chairs and lazy chatter, Lina came up to me and whispered conspiratorially, "I have baby on stove, too!"

"We'll both have a child who could be president!" I congratulated her. Lina smiled politely, uncomprehending, and I mentally kicked myself for allowing my wall to come down that far. Lina would surely ask the others what I had meant. The distance I had established as their teacher and as an American would dissolve when they realized I was one of them, Russian-born and bred, even if I had come here years before them.

∞∞∞∞∞∞∞∞∞∞∞∞∞∞∞∞∞

My spark for mimicry and the learning of languages was inherited from and fanned by *Dyedushka*, my father's father, who lived with us all my growing up years. Dyedushka knew Russian, German, French, Yiddish, Latin, and Italian. His son, my father, smoked and stared absently over our heads, barely speaking even Russian. Dyedushka and I studied every day after school and on weekends, for I was on fire to master his languages and then teach him English, which I was learning in school.

"I need Irina in the kitchen," my mother would complain. Dyedushka always answered, "In a minute, in a minute," turning to me in a loud stage whisper, "Grandparents and grandchildren have a common enemy." He would waggle his ample eyebrows, two furry caterpillars jumping above his dark eyes. After years of my mother's complaining, he simply waggled his eyebrows and the proverb formed silently in my brain. I would nod knowingly. Dyedushska and I had many unspoken conversations. We still do.

As a star English speaker, I was regularly pulled out of class by the high school principal whenever American and British groups came to Tashkent. It didn't hurt that I had developed quite a nice chest and I made sure to wear snug, low-cut tops to show off my cleavage as I translated and embellished.

To the visiting business and government officials, I extolled the brilliant education we young people were receiving — before heading into Tashkent's declining cotton and silk industries. I encouraged the tourists to stop on street corners to taste our regional dish, *plov*, a steamy experience of meat, rice, carrots and garbanzo beans — during which time they and the various cooks could argue about the right knives, and ingredients, and cooking time to add to the authenticity of the occasion.

At first, the Russian tour organizers were unnerved by my voluble willingness to paint my fellow countrymen as over-grown children. As they saw how much the visitors enjoyed my patter, though, I barely had time for school, so great became their demand for me. I had my mother's sharp tongue to thank for my waggish comments — only now do I realize this.

A coquettish smile and a sly lift of the eyebrow, mine more calculating than Dyedushka's hairy oscillations, helped jolly visitors into showering me with money, cigarettes, and gum. Americans loved colorful stories to take home. I wanted them to take me home, and in 1990 the head of the Seattle-Tashkent Sister City Committee and his wife offered.

There was a place in Seattle for a smart, beautiful girl like me, Mr. and Mrs. Spitzer said. With my beloved Dyedushka buried in Tashkent barely a year, Islamists on the rise, and my sister and parents insisting I come with them to Israel, I accepted the Spitzers' offer instantly.

Mr. Spitzer helped me enroll at the University of Washington. He and his family had me over for Shabbat dinners — with eligible Jewish men in attendance each time — before I repaid their kindnesses by falling in love with a penniless UW graduate student in Classics. He was either Axel Hamburg from Hanover or Axel Hanover from Hamburg. It took several weeks for Axel to speak loud enough for me to figure out the correct order.

Axel's glasses fogged when I quoted Chekhov or Tolstoy to him in the original Russian. He thought "not under 21" in America went for sex as well as alcohol, and waited a heroic year before…asking me to remove my shoes upon entering his immaculate apartment. Somehow, he clumsily bedded me, coming over to my place with flowers the next day to apologize. Our marriage was like living with my father again, only this time as his wife.

Yet, Axel Hamburg, half-Jewish as it turned out, helped transform me, Irina Zakashanskaya, to Irene Hamburg. While Axel toiled away on his dissertation, I added to his meager stipend by teaching English as a Second Language. Yes, I over-reached when I wrote my parents that I was now a comfortably married professor. Send us American dollars, they wrote back.

◇◇◇◇◇◇◇◇◇◇◇◇◇◇◇◇◇◇

Initially, I acknowledged my pregnancy only with my students and in the confines of our apartment. At home, I babbled Russian nursery rhymes to my bulge. Axel, bemused in his otherworldly way, gently requested that I teach the bump some German *kinderlieder* too.

Mindful of how an infant might keep us from living the adventuresome life (as if!), Axel, something of a birder, suggested a trip to see bald eagles before we settled down to build our nest. On a Sunday during winter break, 30 weeks into my pregnancy, we set out on Interstate-5 for rural Whatcom County, about three hours north of Seattle.

In December and January, bald eagles feast on washed-up salmon carcasses where the Nooksack River starts as small trickling veins, far from the freeway where cars sprayed black slush onto our windshield. A steady snowfall obscured the snowy dome of the northern-most of the Cascade volcanoes, Mt. Baker, and its neighbor, Mt. Shuksan. Near their bases were the headwaters of the Nooksack.

As we climbed the mountain road, there were no houses or other cars for many miles, and, then, like wraiths, a dozen people with binoculars were milling about in the dim light at an opening above the river.

Axel parked the car, and we gingerly made our way through hat-sized snow doilies to the viewpoint. Hardy birders were taking pictures and remarking on the personalities of the eagles in hushed tones, as if in a sanctified place. Whenever they opened their thermoses, steam fused with the thick, still air. I eagerly accepted a little cup, its warmth dampening my face. In such cold had Dyedushka drunk his chai. His childhood stories of hypothermia, and bedbugs, during Russian winters had alternately thrilled and frightened me.

When dusk turned the pines hazy purple, the birdwatchers walked to their cars, flicked on their headlights and purred back to civilization, until only

Axel and I, in as tight a hug as my big belly would allow, stood absorbing the magnificent violet silence.

My standing around watching the eagles had woken up the baby. Its fluttery movements deep underneath my long underwear and jacket played with my balance. I held tightly onto Axel's arm as we walked to our car. Amazing how much snow had accumulated while we had been watching the eagles.

A sudden onset of complete darkness troubled me. "Axel, drive a little faster," I urged, "just until we get closer to the inhabited areas." When he stepped on the gas pedal, a horrible banging heightened my fear. What on earth? Axel stopped the car in the middle of the road.

The tire chain on the passenger side was tangled, wrapped around the car axle. My Axel worked with his gloves on until, in disgust, he threw them off and, quivering from lying on the cold snow, tried to pull apart metal and wire.

Feeling useless sitting in the car, I got out and told Axel I would walk down the road to look for help, the cold and dark obliterating any clear thinking on our parts.

"Maybe you should stay here," he protested meekly, and I realized he, too, was frightened. I wanted to kick him and scream, "Take charge."

Instead, I stumbled off through the snow, thinking again of my grandfather's tales of Russian winters: peasants burrowing into haystacks when caught by a surprise storm; or drunk revelers shedding clothes until they dropped, naked and delirious, into snowdrifts and eternal sleep.

With a freshening wind, the snowflakes stung my face. My eyes were tiny slits, making the shadows at the edge of the forest hover between representation and abstraction. Bobcats? Evil spirits? I spit three times to ward off anything, taking small comfort in the ancient ritual in which even my worldly Dyedushka had indulged.

I tromped on. Cold seeped through my clothes and into my bones and, I feared, into my baby's tiny home. "Dyedushka," I called out. "Intercede for me. Save us."

A raven coasted silently down onto a snow-covered sign ahead of me and sat there until I could almost touch it, before winging into the woods. How I knew to swipe snow off the sign I cannot tell you, but I did wonder if I was hallucinating because the words were in Russian.

My numb lips moved unwillingly as I read: Build Me a sanctuary that I may dwell among you. Old Believers Church, Services Sundays 9 a.m. and 5 p.m.

Dyedushka had told me about Old Believers, *Staroviery*. In Russia, these breakaway Christians worshipped in secret because they were terrorized and persecuted by the authorities — the only thing we Jews and they had in common, Dyedushka had griped. Old Believers wanted to go back to traditional practices, and most of them left Russia to create isolated communities elsewhere — even in America, in places like Woodburn, Oregon, and, as I was about to learn, Whatcom County, Washington.

I heaved my ponderous body forward, wild with apprehension, praying the driveway would lead me to people who could help. Around a bend I smelled wood smoke. Lights shone through the trees and the winding driveway opened onto a wide expanse, where I saw four parked trucks and a simple white structure.

I knocked on a door and eased it open. A woman in a long skirt and headscarf was in the lobby speaking Russian to three bearded men. She crossed herself when she saw me. Young boys playing nearby with a big empty box looked up, like raccoons in the garbage.

I stammered out my story in frozen English and Russian. The men grabbed coats and roared down the driveway in their trucks. I sank into a chair and wrapped my arms around my stomach, relieved that the baby inside me was safe.

Thank you, Dyedushka, I thought.

Chai?

Da. The woman returned with tea.

Eyes closed, I leaned back into the chair. From time to time my brain registered the sounds of sweeping and of children pushing boxes. I woke up to the roar of lurching trucks. The Russian men stomped in and told me they had cut the tangled tire chains and had escorted Axel to the main road, which was plowed and passable. They would drive me to our car.

The woman pressed a thermos into my hands. I thanked her again and again, *spasiba balshoi*. The children peered at me in silence from their boxes, not returning my weak smile.

Axel got out of our car when he saw us pull up. He put his icy lips on my forehead. *Gottzudanken*, thank God, you're safe.

Thank Dyedushka, I whispered. Axel thought I was talking about the men standing around us. I already did, he said, mildly irritated, sticking out his gloved hand for hearty shakes.

I poured him tea while the bearded men chided us in Russian. Next time bring blankets, thermos, cell phone, they scolded. I nodded dumbly. Exhausted, Axel and I drove west to Interstate-5, feeling utterly foolish at having taken on the elements so unprepared.

Lower back pain kept me from falling asleep in the car. Hours later, at home, I could only pace and try to use the toilet as the pain grew in larger and larger waves. Axel gave me back massages and left a scared message for the midwife. My prolonged flailing through the deep snow had triggered the onset of labor, only neither of us knew that, not having had a baby before.

The midwife showed up to see my body pushing out a baby. She took one look and incautiously blurted out, "Oh, it's too small." She picked up our bedroom phone.

In minutes, orange and red emergency lights were circling in the blackness outside our apartment and through our bedroom window, like whirling heads of my colorfully coiffed Russian ladies.

Once the umbilical cord was snipped, the baby, wrapped in bath towels, disappeared with a medic. The midwife directed another medic to help me squat over a large bowl and push out the placenta.

I wanted to protest, *I don't know this man, and he is watching me expel bloody organs.* Instead I whispered, "Where's Axel?"

"Going to the hospital with your daughter," the midwife crooned.

I wondered dimly: The baby lives? "Tell Axel to name her Safiya." For my grandfather, Salomon, who, no doubt, showed me the way out of the snow. No one appeared to hear me, my voice drowned out by the sirens of the night. From where, the sirens seemed to lament, will come your help now?

◇◇◇◇◇◇◇◇◇◇◇◇◇◇◇◇◇◇◇◇

Axel and I waited for our baby to die. Each day I peered fearfully through the incubator in the ICU at Baby Girl Hamburg and watched her lose a quarter of an ounce, half an ounce, than a whole ounce, which you can't afford to do when you are only 2.8 pounds to begin with.

It had been the right thing, I thought grimly, to have kept my pregnancy from my parents.

The nurses showed me how to place my palm over the little girl's purple head to give her a sense of an enclosing womb. A black strip covered the baby's eyes. Tubes and needles, connected to tiny yellow, blue, and white plastic butterflies, ran over and around her.

Zombie-like, Axel and I scrubbed our hands and donned pale yellow hospital gowns. I steadied myself with a deep breath before stepping through the doors into the unnaturally bright ICU, for in my heart it was snowy and dark. I did not know how to love this rubbery squid-like being, to claim her as my child. The doctors told us that if the baby lived, she might be blind, have bleeds in the brain, respiratory ailments that would cause her to suffocate, or suffer from cerebral palsy.

Those breasts I once nimbly flaunted were now aching cantaloupes. Each hospital visit I sat in a solitary pumping room attached to a solid gray metal sucking machine and watched the light yellow milk squirt into the tiny bottles. I cringed when the nurses showered me with compliments over full bottles. This is the best thing you can do for your daughter, they crowed.

The second week, the nurses insisted we refer to the baby by her name. At their suggestion, Safiya became Sophia. Easier for Americans, they said.

The head of the language program at the college brought Axel and me a basket of wine and pasta and told me my class missed me terribly. When would I come back? Next Monday, I agreed. It had been three weeks already. I would have to face my class and their sympathy at some point.

When I returned, Manya and Fanya were ready with beautiful flowers. The other Russian ladies had platters of piroshky and knishes for me to eat — *pryamo seychas,* right now — to keep up my strength and, of course, more to bring home. Food, the handmaiden of caring. The Ethiopian boys smiled feebly and slid deeper into their jackets. The Mexicans came up to me, pressing my hands into theirs. We are praying for your baby, they said quietly.

I kept glancing at Lina's stomach, which in three weeks had popped right out as if she had a laundry basket shoved up her sweater.

My composure was unquestionable, restrained, no tears. I thought I conducted my first class back with great dignity.

Lina said she very much wanted to see my baby, but, she continued with a nervous smile, it would be bad luck to go to the hospital in her condition. I nodded stiffly and backed away from her and, really, from everything except the routine of classes and hospital visits.

∞∞∞∞∞∞∞∞∞∞∞∞∞∞

Axel and I brought our five-pounder home the week she was to have been born, plunging into a blurry year of relapses and hospital stays, of weary nights during which Sophia's coughing and crying stopped only if I walked her from room to room in our tiny apartment until the first birds began to chirp. I finally sent my parents a photo. "She is so skinny," they wrote back. "You don't have the right foods in your America."

I lost track of my students. Lina drifted away, busy with her older boy, Dima, and the new baby, Leo. I heard she was hired to teach preschool.

For two years, Sophia fought off colds and lung infections. Eagerly, if unsteadily, she began preschool. A day later her teacher took me aside and urged me to get her hearing tested. Axel and I were stunned. How could Sophia have fooled us for so long? How could we have not figured out that she was compensating with her eyes for what her ears were not telling her? Our Sophia's premature arrival had left her profoundly deaf.

"For you, it's just another language to learn." Axel dismissed. For him the confirmation of Sophia's hearing loss was mostly an unwelcome intrusion to his research. Furious at his detachment, I dug for my hidden cigarettes and lit up in front of him, which I knew he would find offensive, before moving out onto the deck to finish my smoke.

I glared at my hands and tried to remember some of the signs Axel and I had seen in class that night. Along with other stricken parents and a few brave grandparents, we had tried to copy the teacher's finger and arms movements — signs for father and for mother and for love you and for cookie. For the first time since bringing our daughter home from the hospital, we exchanged tentative words. Sophia imitated us perfectly, her tiny fingers so much more adept than our hesitant ones. Axel began missing sign classes. Too much, on top of his teaching and research responsibilities, he said. He came to use me as his interpreter for Sophia, who, nevertheless, insisted on shaping her father's fingers and hands to make signs when he was at home, forcing him to communicate, at least with her.

When Lina surprised me with a call, we naturally lapsed into Russian. English was for the kids. "Let's get together," she said.

We met at a playground. Lina's hair was dyed a new red, called "warm comfort," she told me, beaming. I, however, only had eyes for her chubby two-year-old, Leo, who never stopped moving or talking. With legs like tree stumps, Leo made my Sophia look like a fragile reed.

Lina, still as plump and artless as a boiled potato, watched Sophia stagger from swing to pole to climbing toy. Sophia was unable to do much more than lean against the playground equipment when she finally arrived at it, a pleased smile on her face, eyebrows delicately a-wiggle. She stretched her arms out, fingers talking. "Lift me."

Sophia cannot hear, I told Lina, who struggled to put on a good face and, like a Russian mother, hit on, surely, a positive element.

"She will always need you, be close to you." Lina's nose got very red and she wiped her eyes unabashedly. "Sons go away. Daughters stay close."

I hadn't, I thought sullenly.

"That's why I try for girl." She was pregnant again!

"I cry over everything," Lina confessed. "Cereal commercials on TV, I cry." She blew her nose. "Sophia can still be president. She just need interpreter. It can be you."

Lina looked into my soul, then slowly put her palms side by side as if to pray. "Happy and sad lives next door."

The strangest sound ripped from my throat. Lina's big arms were around me and she wouldn't let go. I didn't want her to let go. I didn't wriggle away. Can a captive be freed only by someone not similarly yoked?

When Lina let go, I looked down to see Sophia wrapped around my legs.

"Mama crying? Need a hug?" Sophia signed. I backed onto a picnic table bench and pulled her, my loveable survivor, into my lap. After a time, I pried her off my chest and signed, "Enough sad. Show Mama how to laugh."

I almost dropped her as she fearlessly reared back and threw open her mouth, dazzling me with the exquisiteness of her tiny teeth and tongue, the beautiful, wordless sound of her full-throated glee, an expression of joy that needed no language.

Shura's House

In the denim dawn Robert slipped his hand into Shura's chest. In the dream, his fingers closed around her heart. Not enough to stop it from beating, just enough to make her rub an aching left pectoral when she woke and groggily wonder if she had slept in some awkward way to avoid the youngest boy, all skinny arms and legs, who lay between Darron and herself.

Inert, rotund, self-conscious even while asleep, Darron had one arm draped over his bay window stomach. His cheeks puffed with each exhale. She turned her face away to avoid smelling his rotten sinus breath. She pried out her earplugs. They dulled but could not shut out his snores, a Mack truck stuck in gear. Eyes closed, mind untethered, she had spent the night dreaming of Robert, again, while waking up next to good old Darron. It was a constant and desirable contradiction each morning, a reminder that there was no getting over the affair easily.

Shura peeked around the blinds. The tentative green of April glistened. Easing out of bed, she padded into the kitchen to fill Darron's thermos with coffee and to pack lunches for the three boys. Her fingers trembled.

Yesterday, from Dulles Airport outside Washington, D.C., Robert had left a message on her studio phone.

"Hi Shura, it's Robert Koenig." *Thirty years I've known him and he still gives me his last name.*

"I'm on my way out to Bellingham. My mother's been in a car wreck in which there was a fatality. You can reach me at her house. Hope to talk to you."

So formal, this old high school lover of mine. Shura had stayed home, paid in-state tuition. Robert, a National Merit Scholar, had snared a colossal grant to Harvard and never looked west. Over the years she'd sent him art show opening flyers and birth announcements. He'd sent her his partnership notice in a prestigious Washington, D.C. law firm, the names pinned together by so many commas.

Shura checked the family calendar on the kitchen wall. No lessons, no dental appointments on this day, the vernal equinox. No trace of her movements. Shura kept her twitchy hands in the pockets of her robe as Darron and the boys ran out the front door, stapling kisses on her cheek like roofers with power-tool lips. The luminous spring morning surged with birdsong and comely omens.

She waited, listening for the routine return for a forgotten backpack, the frantic assault on the kitchen table where homework had been left. She waited until they couldn't possibly be coming back, then dug deep to remember the Bellingham phone number, experiencing a familiar mixture of fear and exquisite suspense.

"Koenig residence." She heard his voice, the voice of a highly regarded Securities lawyer. Robert was in charge and not letting his mother answer the phone any more. Too risky, he told Shura. Much of yesterday had been spent fending off insurance agents, local lawyers, and distant friends eager to get reacquainted after reading the newspaper.

Shura offered to come up, the purr in Robert's voice giving her pelvic floor flutters. "Thanks, that would be lovely," he hummed.

Spring in Seattle always holds surprises.

Before heading north, Shura pulled together ingredients for chocolate zucchini bread, her comfort food specialty. There was the wash to hang, too.

Twelve years ago she had been popping out babies like a Pez dispenser. Three boys in four years. She and Darron were artists, too hip to get married and too poor to fix him—or the dryer.

In the backyard of their Alki Point bungalow in West Seattle, she had strung up a laundry line. Each summer, the growing boys chased each other between limp shirts and diapers before exploding out from under billowing sheets. Down came the laundry. No more running around the wash, she yelled. Those clever boys dragged out chairs and boxes, turning towels into fragile walls, pillowcases into undulating hiding places. Come see our fort, they shouted. She dutifully crawled into the clean, soap-sweet smell of their tablecloth tents.

Shura came to love that laundry line and its infinite patterns: blue jeans, contrasting orange T-shirts, dabs of white socks. At the end of the day, she reverently inhaled the sunshine captured in the crunchy towels. A new dryer, bought last year, was used only during the wet, gray winters. *Alas, when a little color on a line would do a body good.*

This spring morning there was no thought to effect. She was in a hurry. Her long fingers flung up jockey shorts, sweatshirts, and baseball pants on the line, revelations to the whippy wind and curious neighbors.

She imagined her artist friends asking, Where are you showing these days? *On my clothesline.* Nothing compelled her to paint since her vow last year to Darron.

Shura checked the kitchen clock and calculated. To be home after school with something baked left her…seven hours to drive 80 miles up and down Interstate-5 and get in a visit to Robert and his mother. After shoveling in warm food, her boys would willingly recount their day, would never think to ask about hers.

Long ago, she had baked brownies in glass pans in the Koenig's small, '50s kitchen. Hovering and ravenous, Robert and his swim team had gouged out warm chunks, chugging glasses of milk. Watching the tumult from the safety of the living room, Mr. Koenig had played with his pipe and pretended to read his academic journals. Mrs. Koenig had darted in from time to time to sponge down the counters and floor and to learn all kinds of teenage tidbits.

◇◇◇◇◇◇◇◇◇◇◇◇◇◇◇◇◇◇◇

An hour-and-a-half after Shura left West Seattle, she pulled her van into the Koenig's driveway, remembering the white Volkswagen bug long ago hauled away. She and Robert had spent much of their senior year in high school finding dark, out-of-the-way places in it.

She knocked. A gray-haired gentleman opened the door. She stared at Robert, breaststroke buff, despite having aged since she saw him last.

He wore a white dress shirt and navy pin-striped pants. He had come directly from his law office on the first plane to Seattle, he told her, and had been wearing the same clothes for two days. She aimed for his cheek and found his lips.

"How's your mother?"

"Shaken up, probably best if we don't dwell on the accident. I'll show you *The Bellingham Herald* later."

Shura dumped her bags on the kitchen table and hugged Mrs. Koenig, a chastened child. The old woman leaned back into her chair, unsteady on her feet, hearing aids wrapped around her ears. *Why was she still driving in the first place?* Shura wondered, while pulling out zucchinis, flour, eggs, chocolate chips, grater, measuring spoons, a leaking bottle of maple syrup.

"I forgot the salad oil. Robert, can you run to the store? Why are my sandals sticking to the floor? Oh, the syrup spilled," Shura babbled, her heart in a race with her jittery fingers.

Robert grabbed a sponge, swiped at the floor and was off. Shura bustled between cupboards. "Don't get up, Mrs. Koenig, just show me. Where is a big mixing bowl?"

The floor might as well have been coated with adhesive. "I think your son spread the syrup around in a fine sheen," Shura complained. She took off her sandals and rinsed them under hot water. "Give me your feet," she entreated, lifting Mrs. Koenig's calves and washing the soles of the old woman's shoes. Shura felt shaking and looked up, worried. Mrs. Koenig was giggling, now rocking with laughter. Shura snickered politely and waited for an explanation.

"Oh, I needed that. I needed a silly moment," Mrs. Koenig sighed, wiping her eyes. "He's been keeping me a prisoner." Shura knew what she meant.

Robert returned with salad oil and lunch. Shura mixed in the final ingredient and slid two loaf pans into the oven with a triumphant cackle. Still on schedule! They spoke of light and inconsequential things until the housecleaner showed up with hugs for Robert and Mrs. Koenig, a nod of her head for Shura, and a frown for the still-sticky floor. A Fed Ex truck pulled in the driveway and a courier delivered a package of jeans and running shoes for Robert from his wife. Robert changed in his old bedroom while answering more phone calls.

To escape the commotion, Shura slipped into the backyard, drawn to Mrs. Koenig's daffodils. Her fingers drifted through the yellow swath as if she were trailing them in water behind a dinghy's stern. She recalled a professor's words: Painting is seeing. The yellow of these flowers could be depicted as gold or sallow margarine or the strident color of egg yolk, she mused. Oddly, the swaying blooms took on the appearance of long, admonishing index fingers: *We know your true colors.*

Tingling with anticipation, and a measure of guilt, she plunged her hands into them as she might break a pool's surface tension. Eyes closed, she turned her face up to the dazzling sun — to blanch any doubts.

Three years ago Robert had told her he was too young to be bored and too old to be chasing 25-year-old secretaries. He had come without his wife to Shura's first show in Washington, D.C. Shura had smiled at him, at the gallery owner, at the guests. She'd inclined her head towards her paintings. "I think there's promise," she said demurely, wondering if he would understand her intent.

He had escorted her back to her hotel room where, with characteristic foresight, he'd pulled out a bottle of Pol Roget from his old law-school brief-case, its corners like bare elbows sticking through a worn sweater.

They sat at either ends of the couch, a distance soon reduced by the champagne.

Unsure at first, their lips pressed and sought until recognition blurred responsibility. Their tongues collided in what she described to him later as a soul kiss—long, and long overdue. Giddy, Shura pulled away.

"Oh," she sighed. "I was so hoping you would do that."

Robert had given her an indulgent smile.

"Wait. Do you have some kind of understanding with your wife?"

"It's alright, Shura. It's okay."

"Have you done this before?"

He laughed, "Shura, I don't know any more what I'm doing than you do."

Well, it wasn't a yes.

"I must take you to Paris sometime," Robert had whispered into her tousled hair as he left her that night. Taking the second room key with him, he'd slipped in the next morning, and the next, on his way to work

Like addicts, they lived and died for word from each other: by email, by post, by phone — dazzling words of surrender and impure thoughts, of discovering how they had imprinted each other, of coming home.

A few months later Robert had flown up for her show in New York.

I want to buy some land in the San Juan Islands, a summer cottage with a key for you and a key for me, he proposed. He called his wife to say he needed an extra day in the city due to complications with a client.

A year into their reunion, an artist friend in Denver alerted Darron to a chummy older man who seemed far more interested in Shura than her art. Darron grew watchful as Shura painted with increasing ferocity, springing from their bed to her studio at all hours of the night.

One early morning Darron slid under her comforter in the studio where she was sleeping. She called him Robert, felt his bulk and said, "I don't make love to pregnant men," instantly regretting her drowsy blunder.

Darron began working out.

Six months later, Shura came home from an exhibit in San Francisco where she and Robert had sipped more champagne, while making love and excuses. Desire was the other side of dissatisfaction, the duality of love, they had assured each other.

In front of the house, Shura had stepped out of the airport cab, and over sodden, wood stilts lying in the driveway. Skateboards and basketballs were chucked into the planters on either side of the entry. The long-missing ice cream scoop was duct-taped to her kitchen mop — a catapult — likely the work of her youngest.

"Hello?" she called, setting down her luggage and peeling off her damp jacket.

Darron, the expansive old Darron, pounded down the stairs, wordlessly escorting her back out into the drizzle. He's been plotting, she thought. *This could be awkward.* In their rambunctious backyard, rife with unfinished projects and weed-filled beds, he picked up her left hand and surprised her.

Two gold bands lay in his right palm.

"I realize we need reminders," Darron's voice shook. "You'll look at this ring and I'll look at my ring and we'll remember we made a promise to each other. I promise to love you and take care of you and raise the boys with you now and forever." He nodded toward her.

Shura looked at Darron, so earnest, so round, his mesomorph body better suited to mushing dog sleds than designing commercial posters. She scanned the tall Douglas firs and omnipresent ferns. She looked at the boy detritus — squirt guns and light sabers — tossed carelessly in the grass. This topsy-turvy tableau of growth was their life, her life.

"I promise to love you and take care of you and raise the boys with you now and forever," she repeated. *Time to release the helium balloons of fantasy. Embrace the life you actually have. You chose it for reasons you may not have given much thought to lately.*

"You know what kissing you is like?" Darron licked his lips. "It's like these donuts I ate as a kid. Those big ones with the soft, creamy stuff inside and you would stick your tongue in the little hole and lick it all in."

Shura assured Darron, the budding poet, she would not stray again. "I've been impulsive and selfish and stupid. I'm done," she pledged. With Robert it was always a promised land. With Darron, a land that held promise.

◇◇◇◇◇◇◇◇◇◇◇◇◇◇◇◇◇◇◇

Now, through the kitchen window, Robert watched Shura in the backyard by the daffodils, the phone cradled between his jaw and shoulder as he wrote down information. His mother, at his elbow, followed his look. He hung up the phone.

"I imagine she must be a temptation to you," Mrs. Koenig said.

He gave a startled nod before tapping on the window and pointing to his watch. Shura scampered in to take out the zucchini bread, the smell of warm chocolate filling the kitchen. The loaves would cool while she and Robert went for a walk.

The wind, which had set her Seattle clothesline bobbing, shooed Bellingham's rainclouds east, revealing a sun so intense it nearly knocked on doors. Mrs. Koenig's neighbor stepped into his front yard. "This is why we live here!" he exulted at Shura and Robert. Others along their route propped open windows and doors. Strangers waved at Shura and Robert, who had always held hands while walking towards Bellingham Bay. They left the road, picking their way around huckleberry bushes and salal.

Like some wild cowboy, the wind rounded up the last bits of cloud and rain. It whooped and threw waves against the rocks. Trees appeared to be tugging free of their roots, and, as if in anchored frustration, flung pinecones and branches through the washed air.

Robert and Shura clambered past creaking Douglas firs to look down on the gnashing water below the cliffs. On the other side of the bay lay flat Eliza Island, a steppingstone onto the forested back of Lummi Island, a gigantic dinosaur in repose.

The woods in which they stood were as wild as when seen by explorer Captain George Vancouver in 1792. No developers had been allowed in with their subdivisions, yet. In high school, Shura and Robert had learned that Captain George named the area after Sir William Bellingham, controller of the storekeepers' accounts for the British Navy. The first inhabitants, the Lummi and Nooksack Indians, called the place Whatcom, *noisy-all-the time,* for the sound of many little waterfalls echoing off the tall trees.

Today, the wind out-roared all sounds. It stampeded through trees and gave Robert and Shura wind-tunnel coiffures.

"This is where I came to write the words for my father's funeral," Robert yelled. "This is my sanctuary." Shura tried to talk but her hair filled her mouth. She felt buffeted by more than just the elements.

Her father, gone nearly nine years, loved charging through the bay's whitecaps in his small sailboat. She remembered her mother's mouth, a taut line of distress, and her voice: Walter, can't you let the sails out a little? Walter, this is not pleasant. Walter, we are going to tip over!

You're such a horse's ass, Walter had laughed.

Shura had agreed with her mother, yet she loved her reckless, black-haired pirate of a father too much to chance being called a horse's ass too. She would lie down on the high side of the sailboat and suck the salty straps of her life preserver.

Robert and Shura climbed away from the edge of the cliff and into the forest. "Let's go a little farther," she suggested, following a faint path, looking for a protected nook. On an even wilder day, years ago, the wind had lassoed a Douglas fir down to the ground, creating just what she was seeking.

Oh! This was much more than she had hoped to find. Off to one side of the path was a small lean-to. Branches had been placed against the trunk's massive base. Shura laughed with delight when she looked into the lean-to. Lustrous fern fronds covered the ground inside, a soft, springy bed big enough for two. A masterpiece! She drew Robert down with her, figuring he, a big-city guy now, wouldn't of his own accord get so close to soil, tree roots, and cobwebs. The musky humus smell calmed her.

"Who could have built this?" Shura asked, taking his silent shrug for discomfort.

The sun wriggled through the lean-to's branches and slithered over their faces. Kisses led to undressing. The world was a mossy womb, a loamy never-never land, no bigger than the length of their bodies. There were no phones, no planes, no fatal accidents. No regrets.

She thought about slipping off the ring Darron had given her. Then again, Robert had never taken off his. She decided to stop thinking. They caressed lines and wrinkles, kissed sags, two smitten high school seniors.

"Other people see you as the age you are now," she whispered. "I see you as every age." She stroked his gray hair. He twirled her salt-and-pepper curls with his fingers. She peeked up at him once, quickly closing her eyes again. His eyes had been wide open, watching her.

"Don't you ever close your eyes during sex?"

"I don't have to fantasize with you, Shura."

The wind died down enough for Shura to hear Robert's rhythmic breathing. She looked at her watch and shook him awake. "I have to leave home to go home," she sighed, scooching out of the lean-to. There was no point in trying to be suave. They laughed at each other's attempts to tug on stockings and pull up boxers, while removing tiny leaves and sticks from their hair and clothes.

"Thank you for coming." Robert's lips were on her ear. "Seeing my mother like this makes me feel old and vulnerable. I have to confess I wander through my days a bit out of sorts, and wonder why I got to this place in life without you."

Shura's voice was pinched. "What's hard for me is this aching sadness of not quite having gotten it right, an awareness that there's a pull-date."

"The immutability of time." His stroke of her cheek turned into a playful pinch. "You know, we're the same age our parents were when we started going out."

Waiting by the front window for their return, Mrs. Koenig, 82-years-smart, saw her son's radiant face and stole back into the kitchen. She feared if she said anything at all she would betray her feelings, or her absent daughter-in-law. She put the kettle on for tea. It would detain Shura a few more minutes.

Mrs. Koenig knew very well what might go on in the forest by the bay. Almost three decades ago she and Dick — Mr. Koenig — had reminded Robert of his future, and that it lay elsewhere. It was not the right time to get serious about anybody. It was good that he and Shura were going to colleges on opposite coasts. It would give them a chance to get to know other people. They expected great things from Robert.

Mrs. Koenig closed her eyes. "Still finding ways to be together," she murmured to herself. At that moment Mrs. Koenig greatly missed her late husband. She gave a tiny tsk. She couldn't talk to Dick, Robert wouldn't tell his wife, and she doubted Shura would say anything to her mate or partner, whatever they called them these days. Three accomplices in an afternoon unrevealed. The kettle screeched.

In the living room, Robert patted the couch for Shura to sit down next to him. He pulled the local newspaper out of his beloved briefcase and pointed to the bold headline: **Driver Runs Red Light in Fatal Accident.**

"Will she be able to drive again?" Shura asked in an undertone.

"No," Robert said. "Her reflexes are slowing. It means a major life change, one of those assisted living places."

The zucchini bread was still warm. Shura packed one loaf for home and turned to hold Mrs. Koenig's veined hands with their blue rivulets.

"I'll come back," she promised. Mrs. Koenig hoped she really would. Robert walked with Shura to the far side of the van for a long hug and a careful kiss his mother couldn't see.

On the drive back to Seattle, Shura's thoughts kept returning to the cunning, little lean-to. It might have been built by transients, or college students, or even some hippie back-to-the-woods type. The past weeks of slanting rain would have deterred even the hardiest soul, though, from tramping about in the woods. She turned the scene over and over in her mind. Those ferns, green and supple, had been freshly cut.

The next morning, after Darron and the boys were launched, Shura began a wash. It was unexpectedly sunny, again, in Seattle. She sorted the previous day's clothes, pressing her face into a crisp towel.

Would that one could hang out longings, misdeeds, and doubts to be dried of their weight and neatly folded away.

She waited for her males' no-return point before calling Robert. She had to know.

"Did you make that lean-to?"

Robert's silence convinced her.

"You did, didn't you?"

"I made a little house for Shura," sang Robert, "where she could come play with me."

She gasped. "But what if I hadn't walked up that path?"

"I would have suggested it." She could hear his naughty smile.

She imagined him dragging branches, careful to keep his office clothes from getting dirty, loafers slipping on the satiny pine needles. She saw Robert stepping back with a sense of satisfaction even the most diligently secured deal could not equal.

A spasm of painful wonder hunched her shoulders and bowed her head. A house. He had built her a house. An artful dwelling in the plant kingdom.

Robert, who lived in a mansion in a wealthy Maryland suburb, earned millions advising corporations. He vacationed in France and Italy with his wife and child, met clients and other East Coast elite for drinks in expensive lounges, drove a Jaguar.

Robert, returning to his backwoods hometown to extract his mother from her accident, had slipped away to his forest refuge and made Shura a place they could call their own. After all these years.

She would meet him there again, she knew. Come boy, she would say through happy tears, stretching a gentle hand to the man of her dreams. Come, sit down next to me. And the boy would love his Shura.

Thickets of Decorum

Three small cuttings traveled west across the Atlantic Ocean among the Swedish war bride's effects. Watching her fuss over the tiny stowaways, her new Yankee husband smiled indulgently. "There are no plants in America?"

Sweden's glaciers glinted in the bride's turquoise eyes as she proclaimed, "These are of my soil and of my soul."

The fifty-year-old family story drifts into Britt's mind. The children of the children of those immigrant plants line shelves along a plate-glass window, next to which the conversation with Mama and her biological offspring is not going well.

Mama is sliding into that all too familiar ice mode, that certain "look" emanating now from the thick glasses the old woman wears, which contort her eyes like carnival mirrors.

Britt is up from California for the weekend at the request of her older brothers, Jonas and Evert. Twelve years after burying their father, the three of them want Mama to leave the family home.

"The assisted living facility has sunny apartments where you could have plants," Evert presses. Jonas and Evert disdain the pots that so crowd Mama's waterfront home. They cause dangerous obstacles in her unsteady path.

"Can I bring all of them?"

Evert sighs. "Mama, you have so many. You'll have to let a few go."

"These are of my soil and of my soul," she intones, for possibly the thousandth time.

"So are we!" Evert pats his chest with both hands. "You let *us* go."

"The plants need me. And Bennett? What's to become of Bennett?"

Evert and Jonas launch into options for their brother's care.

Simple Bennett remembers the tiniest details from their childhood, but can't tell time. What's wrong with Bennett, young Britt had once asked Mama. "*Akh, lillan*, little one, he lives in the past."

Near to bursting with anticipation, Britt remembers hurrying home to tell Mama the right word, the word supplied by the school nurse. Mama's English often failed her. Britt had felt ever so helpful and she liked the way her tongue ticked against her front teeth when she said autistic.

"And this makes you feel better, knowing this name? This provides a cure?" Mama had hissed, hosing her words at Britt like a cold shower.

Britt shivers now, her well-intentioned effort painful, still. After all the years of verbal slaps, Britt pushed back only by moving away for college and staying away. She had to, to save herself. She couldn't save Bennett. Her attention wanders from today's family meeting to Bennett. He is pitching pine cones off the deck, oblivious to the dining room conversation.

Bennett was her great disappointment, Mama had told Britt in a rare and candid phone call after Daddy died. Mama revealed she had "allowed" Britt to happen, hoping to ease her guilt over Bennett with one more normal baby. She'd assumed that after three blue-eyed towheads she'd get a fourth. Only, this new infant was a brown-eyed girl with cardboard beige hair who took after some distant relative *on Daddy's side.* Now Britt's hair, like the boys', has gone bleached beach-house gray.

Bennett, unaware of his shortcomings, smiles at the deck he has cleared. Britt suggested the new game: pine cones could cause their mother to lose her footing. Britt knows Bennett is happy to be Mama's helper. First, Mama asked him to water her outside plants. Then, when her knees started hurting so much she couldn't walk down into the garden, she ordered him to dig up the plants and line the deck with them.

Britt watches him count and recount the parade of pots. "Some are gone!" he shouts.

Bennett does not know that when they visit, Jonas and Evert—fearing the deck might collapse from the weight of all those pots—surreptitiously remove one or two. An effort as productive as rearranging deck chairs on the Titanic, the older boys ruefully joke with Britt. Britt heard this quip at work well over a year ago. Evert's pause for recognition prompts a wan smile from her anyway. Mama's mail is full of garden catalogs, so there are always new pots.

Recently, Mama has asked Bennett to bring plants into the house. Pots are plunked down wherever light comes through the windows. Dead and live plants crowd the entryway, the living room, the kitchen.

This morning, before Jonas and Evert arrived, Britt had watched Mama trundle between the kitchen sink and the rest of the house, watering plants with a juice glass. When Britt offered to help, Mama shooed her off. "It's my exercise."

Jonas, Evert, and Britt plan, among a number of changes, to take away Mama's car before she hurts herself or someone else. A few months back, Jonas kept Mama's car keys for a week after learning that when driving at night, she kept her brights on all the time. Mama reluctantly agreed to limit her driving to day time. Jonas reluctantly returned her keys.

Two weeks in a row, Mama has driven into the ditch alongside the winding road to her house. "Simple miscalculations," she'd chuckled in response to Britt's worried phone calls.

At the scene of the second accident, Jonas, ascertaining she was unhurt, scolded her in front of the tow truck driver and demanded the car keys for good. She dropped them petulantly into his outstretched hand, refusing to reveal where she'd hidden the other set. "Since when do children tell their parents what to do?" she entreated the tow truck driver, who furrowed his forehead for her and diplomatically rolled his eyes for Jonas.

Evert now gets out of his chair at the dining room table and paces in front of Mama. "I know this is difficult for you to hear."

Difficult for me, too, Britt wants to say, but assumes her role of unassuming spectator as the dining room back-and-forth intensifies among the older boys and Mama. Britt feels safer on the sidelines, out of everyone's sightlines, especially Mama's. Duncan, Britt's ex, once asked what word best described her relationship with her mother. "Dutiful," she'd returned.

Mama had taught young Britt to make *pepparkakkar* and *glasmästers sill,* ginger cookies and pickled herring. She'd showed her how to sew initials on pillowcases, ripping out Britt's hard-won stitches if they weren't tiny enough. Britt had absorbed Mama's tight-lipped monologues: Daddy lets the boys run wild. Americans are loud and déclassé. They've forgotten the earth claims them not the other way around. Everything Swedish is better.

Bennett ambles in from the deck, surprised to see his siblings. "What are you doing here?"

Jonas, first-born and executor of Mama's estate, takes the lead. "Mama needs to be in a safe place, Bennett."

Bennett scrunches up his brow. "Where Daddy went?"

Jonas and Evert look at Britt. "He means heaven," she translates.

With a fatherly smile, Jonas inclines his head. "Bennett, you enjoy your friends at the center, right? You are safe and looked after. You get a wonderful warm lunch each day, right? You get to ride on a special bus, right?"

Bennett nods slowly. "Right. Right. Right."

Jonas interrupts him. "We want some people to look after Mama the same way."

Britt's insides cringe on her mother's behalf. Mama sits in displeased silence. "Bennett, you would get to stay at a wonderful place too, and be close to your friends." Jonas claps his hands, applauding this scenario.

"Are you quite finished?" Mama abandons her struggle for self-control.

"Mama, at least take a look," pleads Evert, second-born and the negotiator. "Britt's come all the way from California to go see it with you. Let's go today."

Mama faces Britt, who feels a bubble of resentment at Evert for making her a reason for this outing. Somehow she always ends up a thorn in Mama's side.

"Let's go today," Bennett suggests. "Let's go today."

Mama turns toward the window. Bellingham Bay is dotted with racing sailboats, although it is doubtful she can see them. "I'd have to leave this lovely view," she laments. "We'll have to see. If I go there and don't like it, we should drop this foolishness. I'm really fine where I am."

Jonas seizes the apparition of victory. "You'll be pleasantly surprised. Britt will drive you and we'll meet you there."

With the older boys gone, the cinch around Britt's lungs loosens and she sighs deeply. Britt looks through the living room's plants to the colossal Douglas firs running down the property line. How noble, how straight they stand. When the family moved in, she and the trees were equal in height. Because she likes to believe the same force flows through her and the trees, she lifts up her shoulders and spine in solidarity. This time of year the firs cast shadows over the blueberry bushes she and Mama used to pick.

Britt remembers Mama calling her outside for summer's first *smultron*, wild strawberries, "Quick, into your mouth before the boys see." Mama would let Britt cut roses for her own room, the two of them nestling their faces together to sniff the delicate bouquets.

Mama had spoken Swedish with the kids until they started elementary school. The day they were teased for their halting English, Jonas, Evert, and Britt unequivocally stopped speaking Swedish. Britt can't recall if Mama was ever upset at their boycott of her native tongue. Everything with her was so indirect.

Still is, Britt corrects herself, thinking of the just-completed circular exchange amongst the boys and Mama. So many years of trying to figure out what Mama really meant, except, of course, around etiquette. No enigmas there. Mama hushed them for singing at the table, insisted they write thank you notes moments after opening a gift. Good form at all costs, Mama always urged. If one needed to cry, it was best done behind a closed bathroom door, faucets turned on full throttle.

Mama creeps to the refrigerator to get lunch. Bennett goes back outside on the deck and begins rocking. Britt comes up behind Mama and looks over the old woman's stooped shoulders. The refrigerator contains expired contents and bowls topped with greenish coatings.

Britt reaches around Mama to close the refrigerator door. "I'm taking you and Bennett out to lunch. My treat. I never get to do this."

Mama thinks this is frivolous. She squeezes her lips together. The session with Jonas and Evert has worn her out, though.

"So long as you let me make dinner," Mama bargains. Britt has no intention of eating anything currently in the house. She will stop at the store after the tour of the assisted living facility and get groceries for the three of them.

◇◇◇◇◇◇◇◇◇◇◇◇◇◇◇◇◇

The boys and Britt surround Mama like security agents when they enter the Four Freedoms House. The place is pleasant enough. Britt reads the plaque in the entryway: Freedom of Worship, Freedom from Fear, Freedom from Want, Freedom of Speech. It doesn't smell of old people and it's not overly warm, although warmth might be helpful given the conversation's plummeting temperature between Mama and the matronly Four Freedoms guide, Marie.

"My children insisted I attend this tour," says Mama, crossing her arms.

"They mean well." Marie flashes an understanding smile at Jonas, Evert, and Britt. *I hear this all the time.*

Mama stares at Marie. "Hitler meant well."

Bennett echoes this unfortunate phrase, over and over.

Marie ignores Mama's cold blast and skates forward, showing two tiny apartments. She tries to defrost Mama with light-hearted chatter. Resourceful Marie finds a bowl of mints and silences Bennett by transferring several into his hand. "*Tyst på mun, så får du söcker,*" Mama murmurs. Britt knows Mama also uses this strategy on Bennett: Shut your mouth and you'll get some sugar. Marie is not to be underestimated, Britt allows.

Marie leads them into a large greenhouse. "You grow African violets here?" Mama reaches out to stroke the dark, velvety leaves. "Mine always died, no matter how much I talked to them." Marie goes into detail about weekly visits from a master gardener. "Something to take under consideration," Mama concedes.

They walk past a large room filled with chatting residents engrossed in cards and board games. "All these old people," Mama says in wonderment, as if seeing a species thought to have died off long ago. She looks at herself in a large hall mirror. For verification, Britt imagines. "*Ålderdöm*, old age," Mama whispers. "What a thing to do to a little girl."

When Marie proffers an application packet, Mama nods dismissively at Jonas. "This was his idea." Mama neither returns Marie's wave nor acknowledges the hopeful grin Marie gives Jonas, Evert, and Britt.

◇◇◇◇◇◇◇◇◇◇◇◇◇◇◇◇◇◇

Mama asks Bennett to carry plates, napkins and silverware to the dinner table. Britt hears him croon, "The fork is never right, the fork is never right, the fork is never right," as he comes to each place setting.

"Who shall we have join us tonight, Bennett?" Mama wonders.

He wanders over to the plants. "*Peragonia?*"

"*Bra, bra*, good, good."

He carefully sets a magenta geranium in a chair at the table.

"Aaaannnd…Christmas cactus," he decides, lifting a giant pot into another empty chair at the table. Britt is glad that Jonas and Evert are not around.

After dinner, prepared by Britt, Mama and Bennett drift over to the sofa to watch TV while Britt washes dishes. Britt scrubs down the counters and puts a couple of dead plants in the trash, relieved to have created a little space without incident.

She goes over to the sofa and coaxes Bennett out of his sandals. Earlier, Britt noticed his lengthy toenails. He yields to her clipper. "You could harvest wheat with these," she teases, holding up two clipped nails, tiny gray parentheses. Mama sniggers.

Britt savors the cozy moment, pleased at having recognized its worth. It has taken her plenty of heart ache and a little therapy to get to this place of living more mindfully.

For too many years, unconcerned by the perils of time, Britt, a copy editor for the *Sacramento Bee*, had spent long hours pursuing reportorial inconsistencies rather than interactions with Duncan and their son Brian. Duncan had been the one who'd helped in Brian's classroom or carpooled with the other Little League parents. Britt was always needed to help with a breaking story or was up against a deadline, delaying or keeping her from attending some milestone in young Brian's life.

The three of them grew testy and distant. Still, she had been surprised when, as Duncan and she worked out a separation agreement, Brian, flesh of her flesh, asked her to cut him loose. Like one of Mama's cuttings. Brian wanted to live at his father's. At that moment Britt had known she'd fooled only herself. She *had* been aloof. She *had* put job before family. Duncan's pleas for better communication from her had not been attempts to control. As the old antagonisms have cooled, Britt has started attending Brian's soccer games and going with him and Duncan for pizza afterwards.

Bennett rises. "I'm tired."

"I'll tuck you in," Britt offers. She waits outside his door while he undresses. The creak of the bedsprings cues her to come in and sit down next to him. Bennett clasps his hands around hers. Mama had always sat like this on the edge of their beds and recited prayers.

Bennett starts, "*Gud som haver barnen kär, Se på mig som liten är, Vart jag mig i världen vänder, Står min lycka i Gud's händer.*" God who holds children dear, look down on little me. Wherever I go in this world, my luck rests in Your hands.

Britt mulls over the old words. Mama had always insisted, "You make your own luck." Mixed messages. Mixed-up Britt.

Bennett curls into his pillow. "You finish."

"*Lyckan kommer, lyckan går, Den som älskar, lyckan får.*" Luck comes and luck goes. The one who loves, finds luck.

Bennett's eyes pop open. "You said it wrong." It was true. She had changed the last line years ago when she began reciting it with Brian. The original went *Den Gud älskar, lyckan får.* The one whom God loves, finds luck. Britt never believed good fortune was a serendipitous, divine embrace away.

Later, Britt lies awake in Mama's stuffy guest room, wondering if Duncan tucks Brian into bed. Britt hasn't slept in Mama's house for years. Duncan could not stomach the dusty piles of papers and books, the toothpaste-spattered bathroom mirrors, Bennett's endless repetitions. When they were still together and visited, Duncan, Britt, and Brian had stayed in a nearby bed-and-breakfast. Britt refused to jab back at Mama's pointed comments about rejecting home hospitality. "Otherwise known as home hostility," Britt had whispered grimly in Duncan's ear.

Britt cracks a window in the bedroom and fidgets some more. She could have been a more ministering daughter. She knows very well she has let the burden of Mama's care fall on Jonas' and Evert's shoulders. Had she been more attuned to the situation, she would have seen sooner the need to relocate Mama and Bennett.

Blurry images float through her brain. On the edge of sleep, a sound breaks the dreamy stream. She hears heavy footsteps pad down the hall to Mama's bedroom.

Britt waits in the dark. Minutes stretch like a taut bowstring before she tiptoes down the hall. In Mama's bedroom, the weak nightlight illuminates a big form wrapped around a tiny one. It could have been her parents once again in the bed. Britt's nose starts to run, her eyes sting. Now for sure she cannot sleep.

Once, she too sought refuge from scary night shadows in Bennett's big arms. Mama would pry them loose in the morning, chiding, "Britt, you are too old for this."

◇◇◇◇◇◇◇◇◇◇◇◇◇◇◇◇◇◇

Britt tells Bennett to go outside for the Sunday morning paper. She turns to Mama at the table. "Does Bennett sleepwalk?"

"Since he was a little boy."

Britt must have forgotten this. She is unsure why she wants to lay bare her disapproval. "Mama, Bennett's a man now. It doesn't seem healthy for him to sleep in the same bed as you." Britt doesn't know if she is protecting or seeking revenge.

"Britt, there is absolutely nothing wrong with him coming into my bed. Bennett seeks warmth and companionship." Mama's mouth quivers oddly. Britt waits out a long, strained pause.

"And, to be frank, so do I." Mama looks into her lap at her hands.

What an astonishing admittance from the Nordic queen. To name what she needs! Might there even come a time when Mama asks for what she wants, Britt marvels to herself. It has taken far too long for her, Britt, to say what is right for her and what is not. She is learning how, and, now, maybe Mama, too?

Britt hacks her way through thickets of decorum to plant an awkward kiss on Mama's forehead. Mama acts as if nothing of the sort has just happened. Britt looks away. Helping someone keep their dignity doesn't always feel dignified.

Cell phone in hand, Britt wanders down into Mama's neglected garden. The wild strawberries have overrun everything. The opportunistic lust for life, surging through everything that grows, is never more apparent than in this wild backyard. Someone, probably Bennett, in an attempt to water the farthest corners of the garden, has used the hose like a scythe, flattening several rose bushes.

Britt closes her eyes to the overgrown garden's summer revelry and reflects. She has a month of sick leave accumulated at work. Having come so close to losing her own son, she understands the pain of separation in a way Jonas and Evert can't. They and their lovely wives and their lovely children have never not lived together.

She won't go along with a plan that will wrest Bennett from Mama. Their enmeshed relationship has gone on so long, it is hard to say where Mama ends and Bennett begins, where Bennett's hand stops and Mama's starts.

When Britt opens her eyes, sailboats, their spinnakers like tiny gems, are rounding a distant island in a final leg of the weekend race. She puffs up her own cheeks and blows out her indecision.

Britt dials, waking her son. "Good morning Brian." There is a sleepy "Yeah?" "Mormor and Bennett need me a lot right now. I want to stay up here a little longer. Are you okay with me being gone a few weeks while I sort things out?" His yawn and a languid, "Sure, Mom," make her want to reach through the phone to stroke his rumpled morning hair, to stick her nose into the loose nightshirt full of his snug bed smell.

Bennett is engrossed in the comics and does not hear the car pull into the driveway. Mama and Britt stiffen — Jonas and Evert are back for Round Two.

Britt eases out the front door and engages them in a surprising conversation. When the men come in, it is without their usual stomp and good cheer. They are not happy that Britt has launched an offensive of her own.

The brothers, realtors in the same firm, have made initial moves toward putting Mama's house on the market. They know they will get an amount of money astronomically larger than its original price almost fifty years ago. The money will cover Mama's and Bennett's care and still leave a chunk of change someday for themselves and Britt. What they argue out loud is something else.

"What happens when you go home?" Jonas challenges Britt.

"If I bring someone in and have them work side-by-side with me and Mama, she'll get to know them. By the time I go home, she'll feel less threatened about it because the person won't be a stranger any more." At least Britt hopes to God this is how it will play out, hopes luck will find her. "I'll fly up twice a month on weekends after my leave runs out."

Jonas shakes his head. "You're not being realistic."

Mama motions everyone over to the table where she is finishing her coffee. Since the five of them are together, she says, she has an announcement. Her eyes, behind those glasses, bore into any miscreant who dares not make sense. Jonas and Evert cautiously lower themselves into the dining room chairs. Bennett puts the comics aside to stand behind Mama as if posing for a picture. The foursome turn toward Mama the way plants turn to the sun.

"I don't want to be buried. I want my ashes spread on the garden."

Jonas clears his throat. "Mama, we're here to talk about your life, where you'll be spending good times ahead."

Mama flicks her wrist. "That matter is closed. My daughter is here."

With a small cough, Britt covers up what was nearly a sarcastic laugh: enlisted by Mama when it becomes strategically necessary. This bold redrawing of the boundaries puts Mama, Bennett, and her on one side. Jonas and Evert glare at them from a neighboring country.

Britt seizes her new status. "Bennett, help me move a few plants out to the deck. We're going to make the kitchen floor sparkle." Bennett follows her, a wiggly puppy. "Sparkle. Okey-dokey. Sparkle."

Bennett's easy acquiescence trips in Britt an uneasy observation. While Mama says she wants what's best for Bennett, his subservience has given the old woman a last bit of control over something. Behind her, Britt hears Mama's sharp intake of breath each time Bennett opens the screen door. They are disassembling Mama's protective mantle of existence, pot by pot. If she turns to face the woman, Britt fears her own wobbly resolve will wither.

Britt heads for Mama's broom closet, around the corner from the kitchen. She reaches for a mop and bucket. An odd sound causes her to peer into the bucket.

Still at the table, Jonas and Evert do not see Britt's stealthy reach downward. She picks out the second set of car keys from the bucket and stashes them in her back pants pocket.

A Foot in Each Country

Tiny as a mint, the music director asks nervous questions, wants to know how long we've been moving pianos.

Diego, Yermy, and I are moving a twelve-foot Kawai grand piano from a synagogue's sanctuary to its gymnasium on Vancouver, B.C.'s religion row, where the Sufis, Buddhists, Methodists, Catholics, and Jews line up in imposing edifices along Oak Street like a spiritual smorgasbord.

Diego is underneath the shiny, black Kawai, loosening the pedals. Yermy, our boss, waits for me to slide a support, called a third leg, under the big body.

"How many moves do you do in a day?"

"This is our seventh, and last," I say into the instrument. I wish the woman would quit distracting us. Her flitting about stops when she notices the missing fingers on Yermy's right hand.

"Have you ever had accidents?"

Oddly, Yermy says nothing. What I really want to do is bat her away. She'll back off with a little fast talk. "Had a few close calls. Nearly dropped a piano from a third floor apartment. Was coming down nice and smooth when one of the winches gave way. Sucker came down on its side instead of horizontal. No harm done." Her look says she can't believe no harm was done and, for emphasis, she flips a graying pony tail off her shoulders before petulantly crossing her little-girl arms. She retreats towards the sanctuary doors.

Yermy and I debate whether we need to bring the spider dolly on which the piano sits. Diego, a Humpty Dumpty-shaped tough guy, makes the decision for us by slamming the Y-shaped dolly closed. With no visible effort, he hoists the humungous metal support onto his shoulders and heads for the truck. When he returns, the three of us ease the grand down the outside ramp. That's 1400 pounds of wood, strings, and metal. Too close to the concrete wall and you lose a hand between the wall and the piano. If the other guys aren't braking the weight slowly, you could get crushed. You're dependent on the others and dependent on your own strength and wits. We get the piano into the truck, and the three of us hop into the cab.

The music director waves. "I'll meet you over there." She acts like we can't do this without her either, and helicopters over to the adjacent gymnasium, motioning to us the whole time. We chug across the parking lot behind her.

Yermy wants to know how old we think the music director is.

"Not your type, man," Diego sniffs.

"Woman with job my type."

I guess early forties.

We roll the piano out of the truck and into a gym filled with middle-aged ladies, arms full of candles and cloth napkins, decorating dozens and dozens of tables. Shit, the stage is on risers. We decide to forego the dolly. We will roll the piano up our ramp and onto the stage, a standard three-man assault.

Heading back to the truck for the ramp, I stop at a poster of the evening's entertainment, an impersonator. In between the man's painted black eyebrows and painted black mustache, there's a pair of iconic wire-rimmed glasses. The actor poses insouciantly in a cut-away suit atop a piano. I look over at the stage again and notice what I did not see the first time: a potted palm, an overstuffed armchair and a small table on which sit a replica of a phone and a wooden radio from the 1930s—my great-grandfather's office.

Upon learning my last name, Yermy decided I was related to Karl the way Americans assume I might be related to Groucho. "Marx! Same last name! What kind name Groucho?" Yermy wondered, dismissive. My last name and Yermy's first name, imposed on us by our forebears, created an empathetic bond. "My *mishegene* mother give me countryside name from 1800s — Yermolai. Who names Jewish kid Yermolai? Nine months in Jewish woman's belly and she thinks name Yermolai fool world. Bah!" His hands smacked his cheeks. "*Zhidovskaya morda.*" Jewish mug.

For a time I enjoyed the reverent reactions when I admitted Groucho was my great-grandfather. I stopped the revelations after people expected me to hold forth with salacious family stories or to ad lib nonstop or to know every-thing about the actors and movies of that madcap era. A brief fling with my mother's last name, Meiselman, mouse catcher, provided a different set of indignities. I went back to Marx.

Yermy checks the pedals and keys. I walk off the stage with paperwork and over to the music director. "What's the event tonight?"

"A fundraiser."

"Who's the entertainer?"

"Some actor from Los Angeles. Howard something, impersonating Groucho Marx. He's going to jolly people into forking out big money for the temple remodel."

The music director wants us to return at midnight to move the piano back into the sanctuary. There is a volleyball tournament in the gym the next morning. Holding the synagogue's event in the gym instead of a fancy hotel is a big money saver, she tells me. "Even with paying you overtime." She watches Yermy, still on the stage, play an eight-fingered version of "Moscow Nights."

"Do you play piano too?"

"That's the last thing I want to do when I get home at night."

"How did he lose his fingers?"

The one time I asked Yermy, he growled, "Long, stupid story." Never got an answer and never thought about asking again. That gives me room to extemporize. I give the music director a practiced, pained look. "A real tragedy. He trained for years to be a concert pianist." Her eyes beg for the punch line. "Russian mafia," I whisper. I've been asked about Yermy's hand enough times to have constructed several creative comebacks. Maybe improvisation genes have trickled down to me.

The music director gasps, bringing her left hand up over her mouth. This allows me to see she is not wearing a wedding ring. I'm mildly interested in her, knowing that Yermy is interested. When you're twenty-eight, it's natural to seek ways to undermine your older boss. The music director's pathetic concentration on Yermy forces me to rethink causing any mischief.

I turn my attention to the anticipatory activity in the gym. Custodians are heaving chairs around the tables. A sweaty caterer is directing a clump of young girls wearing tight white T-shirts and short black skirts in wine bottle distribution. A couple of dolled-up old ladies come in, hours early, and assume Yermy is the man. They sway up to the stage. "Are you our evening's entertainment?" "Are you single?" Yermy shoots back. They are captivated. To live as unencumbered as Yermy—there is something to strive for.

I wave Diego over from the water fountain. He doesn't know who Groucho Marx is and doesn't care. No way does he want to come back for a late-night pickup. He has a pretty little wife at home and two pretty baby girls. He hitches up his pants. "I'm gonna go home and make a son." Yermy and I can probably get a couple of strong volunteers at the event to help us push the Kawai into the truck and back into the synagogue. Yermy is not wedded to liability rules.

When Yermy and I pass the poster on our way out, I figure, who's he going to tell, and explain that I am this man's great-grandson.

Yermy frowns. "This Groucho?"

Like he'd been thinking of a different one? I want to return for the show. I am curious to see how an actor will portray my great-grandfather. Yermy is up for the adventure and the opportunity to further flirt with Veronica Dash, the music director. Dash as in Dashilevsky, Yermy divulges.

I drive Diego and Yermy to the piano store and use the truck to drive myself home. I have two hours before I need to pick up Yermy from the apartment he shares with his elderly parents.

In the shower, I mull over how unforgivably little I know about Groucho. My father never knew Groucho because that's the way *his* father, Groucho's son, wanted it. The notoriety, the money, the wives, the resentments all made for glorious gossip and gawd-awful family dynamics. Like his father before him, my father detested any connection with the Marx cosmos.

After my grandfather died, before I was born, Dad dug up and stomped on what was left of his Jewish roots and his tenuous connection to the entertainment industry by going into the stationery business. He married his receptionist, my mother, an escaped Catholic. I've been mostly a nothing, though Yermy and I ventured out to a community Seder in Vancouver this year.

Yermy's family came to British Columbia when Russian Jews were the refugee darlings of the '90s. Smart, pushy, devious, they require you to sit down at their meal table and only get up four hours and a boat-load of vodka later. There are cigarettes between each course. The black-hat Seder Yermy and I attended lasted longer than a Russian meal and Yermy drank everyone under the table — no contest, they served Manischewitz. Yermy's part Jewish too. He likes to remind me: "In Russia we say, 'Shake family tree and out will fall *Zhid.*" Jew.

Before getting into my evening clothes, I lift barbells, a set I bought from Yermy. He operates as a pawnbroker on the side, mostly for Russians in Vancouver. The back of the piano store is loaded with TVs, bikes, and tools, their origin unquestioned.

In fact, I came in the store looking to buy some used weights and noticed the Help Wanted sign in the window. What kind of help? Yermy responded with a few questions of his own, before launching into a lecture about how I should go back to college. Nah, college had been wasted on me, I told him. I never graduated. Spent most of my time in the athletic building's weight room or reading *The New York Times*. Yermy was perplexed by my unremarkable achievements, my underwhelming job experience. A nearly depleted trust-fund that had financed my past, desultory life was not information I wished to share.

Moving pianos seemed heroic, environment altering. Not so far removed from weight lifting, it appealed to my growing need to do something detectable.

Yermy called me "spoiled American Jew" and said lucky for me one of his young grunts had quit. His offer of cash wages meant I didn't need to hassle with a work permit for what I thought was going to be a pretty short-term arrangement. That was two years ago.

Yermy comes out of his apartment building in a double-breasted suit, intent on increasing the sartorial quotient of tonight's event. His hair's slicked back like he's going on stage. I notice the bulge in his suit pocket. "No camera!" I yell and punch his arm. Two weeks ago he'd snuck it into the symphony hall where earlier we had moved a monster Bösendorfer. The stage manager, a Russian, got us tickets to hear the pianist, Vadim Arpanovich. As Vadim took his final bow, Yermy pulled out the camera. "You can't take pictures in here," I hissed. "I got flash, *nyet probleme*," he hissed back.

Yermy makes a show of leaving the camera in the truck's cab when we arrive at the synagogue. In the gym, hundreds of people in fancy dresses and nice suits are laughing and talking and drinking. The craziest thing jumps into my head: a Bible story. A king sends his spell-maker to go curse the Jews, but when the magician steps out to the vista point overlooking thousands of Israelite tents and animals and people, he is transformed by the scene and issues a blessing.

The gym lights have been dimmed in deference to candles. Shiny decorations and twinkling lights are strung between potted palms. The festive glow makes me inexplicably happy. This is how a community gathers. My tribe's having a party, and one should never underestimate the power of a good party.

Yermy's eyes widen. The music director is wearing a low-cut gown. He starts in slaying her with Yermese. "How beautiful you look, like 'Midnight Sonata'."

The woman goes so red I think she might cry. "It's 'Moonlight Sonata'." She motions to the bar. "Help yourself."

"I get you back," Yermy promises her. I wander, smiling absently at all these beautiful people, potentially my beautiful people if I can get past my father's imprinted concealment. I can't shake my self-imposed observer status and I wish someone would invite me to sing our people's song. Yermy isn't troubled about jumping into anything. His irrepressible take on the world and his inventive self-love make him a truer heir to my great-grandfather than me.

An auctioneer encourages everyone to enjoy the kosher wines, knowing it will loosen tongues and billfolds. Welcoming remarks are followed by a frenzy of bids on resort packages and island getaways. Yermy and Veronica park themselves at a stand-up café table and laugh and talk, shooing me away when I come near.

A grandiose introduction from the auctioneer brings a glittery-jacketed pianist on stage. He plays big chords and flashy traveling music for an approaching actor, who has expertly recreated Groucho's lope and slight hunch. Howard Something gets us guffawing instantly. His timing is perfect, an intelligent humor laced with anecdotes from Groucho's life: the FBI had my great-grandfather in its sights for his ribald take on American government; cartoon character Bugs Bunny quoted Groucho between chomps on a carrot.

The auctioneer retakes the stage and puts his arm around Groucho. They're yukking it up together for the audience. The auctioneer asks Groucho if he's ever thought about time travel. Howard frowns, like *This isn't in the script.*

"Ever wondered what your great-grandkids would look like?"

Howard shrugs. *Ok, I'll play.*

I'm looking for an exit or a handy pit in the gym floor.

"Who will start off by giving me $100 to introduce Groucho to a relative he never thought he'd meet?" The guests' heads look up and around, like a field of prairie dogs. A table raises its paddle. "$200 to help Groucho step into the future." The bidding goes on. I can see people eyeing the program, looking for the item number and not finding it. A trembling has begun in my shoes and I fear if I move, I will topple, like a felled tree. The auctioneer and Howard dish back and forth, bringing the figure up to $800, $900, $1,000.

"Ladies and Gentlemen, please welcome Groucho Marx's great-grandson, Eric Marx." Veronica and Yermy pop out of nowhere and escort me to the stage. There is expectant murmuring and applause, while Howard locks onto me with a gaze worthy of a high priest. "You're Robert's boy," he says under his breath. I nod. The guy would know the family. I sense that I am to be cut into little pieces and served to the gathered guests, because if there is one thing that displeases Groucho/Howard it is to be upstaged. I become the target of my great-grandfather's wicked wit.

"I never forget a face, but in your case, I'll be glad to make an exception," Howard quotes Groucho and the audience goes wild. He pokes me. "Why'd they hire *you*?"

"To move the piano." I feel sick. Sweat is blasting out of my forehead. I try to make a crack back but cannot be funny if my life depended on it. There are a few polite titters from the audience. The auctioneer and Howard proceed to verbally pummel me. With each humorous, knife-twisting salvo, I cringe further and further over, turning into what feels like a drooling knuckle-dragger.

I'm signaled to leave. I steel myself to walk slowly and suavely off the stage to where Yermy is flashing me a peace sign. "It's *mitzvah* to be an idiot. How much money you raised!"

I want to bash in his face. "How do you even know the word *mitzvah*?"

"Veronica tell me."

"And you told her who I was, right? You fucking buttinski." I imagine the dollar signs that oscillated on Veronica's eyeballs, like Vegas slots, when Yermy disclosed my connection to Groucho.

Yermy whips out his camera. He wants a photo of Howard and himself, of Howard and me. I flip him off and march to the bar in a wordless column of rage. I drink diligently, shaking hands with congregants and getting slapped on the back.

A dessert auction follows. One table insists I eat some of the cake they win. By the second bite, the usual insufferable questions about the Marx Brothers prompts me to leave. I head for the stage and lurk behind it.

Howard and his lounge lizard pianist find me. They're all chatty now and wanting to make up. They're getting ready to drive to Seattle, where they will spend the night before flying back to L.A. This is their first Canadian gig, and they want to get pictures standing at the Canadian-U.S. border's Peace Arch Park, a foot in each country. The backed-up traffic coming into British Columbia had left them no time for photos. Southbound, at this time of night, they figure there will be brilliant floodlights and no lines.

Howard thrusts his hand in my direction. "No harm meant, pal. It's show biz. Last name's Losi." I try out the name.

"Not Jewish, Sicilian. We probably had relatives on the same boat." Howard Losi wants my contact information for a "project" he's working on with "the family," which means my Uncle Ben, who still lives in L.A., a Groucho grandkid. The grandkids don't talk to each other. Since Howard is not family, he's probably getting an earful from old Uncle Benny.

Not soon enough for me, the auction ends and the guests line up at the coat check. The synagogue's worker bees are tallying up the night's take. The girls in white and black droop over messy tables and trash bags.

I want to get the piano out and go home. Unsteadily, I thread my way through the crowd towards Yermy. He still is chatting up Veronica, her face unguarded and inviting. She touches Yermy's hand lightly. "How do you play the piano minus two fingers?"

"Piece piroshky."

"You mean piece of cake?" She laughs indulgently and overlong. Veronica has followed the auctioneer's directive and enjoyed the fruit of the vine. Yermy ignores my dead trout look. He's the boss. When he's in a rush, I'm in a rush. When he's turning on the charm for a music director, I'm left sizing up who I can strong arm into helping me move the piano.

If I can't be an entertainer in the best tradition of Groucho or a master flirt like Yermy, I decide to be the best piano mover I can be. I go to the truck for the pads and blankets. When I return, Yermy is mounting the stairs to the stage, holding Veronica's hand. He sits down at the Kawai and warbles something in Russian while I do a slow burn. I stand below him on the gym floor and shove my fists into my pants pockets.

"My grandparents were Russian," Veronica giggles. "I think they might even have sung that song." She leans on the closed piano top, a miniature cleavage inches from Yermy's face. Up she goes on top of the piano in front of Yermy, lying head in hand on elbow à la Groucho. "I've always wanted to do this," she trills. There are hoots from the remaining guests. I want to wave a giant magician's handkerchief and shout, "Watch carefully as I extract this instrument from the gymnasium." I just want to friggin' go home.

I round up a few big guys and they follow me over to the stage. Veronica, suddenly self-conscious when surrounded, descends from the piano. She advises Yermy that she will go look for our check. Yermy glares at me, furious at the interruption, at my initiative.

"What's with you and Lady Bountiful? She's desperate." I needle.

Yermy pulls himself up and looks down his long Semitic nose at me. "Is very Russian, this desperation."

We get the Kawai into the truck, Yermy and I not bothering to hide our animosity. We drive over to the synagogue entrance in ominous silence. The late hour and the wine we've drunk make pushing the black mother up the ramp into the synagogue sanctuary an ordeal. A warning voice keeps pecking at me to "Go slow and no one will get hurt."

The spider dolly is jammed into an I-shape, Diego's work from the afternoon move. I am not strong enough to push it wider apart. Yermy grabs a mallet and I hold the middle of the dolly so he can give it a whack. A slow awareness that Yermy's reflexes might be impaired by anger and alcohol comes right before the excruciating pain of thick metal slamming my knuckles from the front and into the equally thick metal dolly arm behind. The pain is beyond comprehension. Blood pours out over the dolly and onto the sanctuary rug.

Yermy looks like a scared little boy. "*Bozhemoy.*" My God. He swings the mallet and hits the dolly arm the other way, releasing my smashed hand. I roll onto my back and, remembering some vague medical advice, lift an oozing, red scepter into the air before closing my eyes. I can feel blood running down my arm. I hear a babble of voices and Veronica screaming for someone to call emergency services. Something soft is slid under my head. I know if I open my eyes, I will throw up.

The medics come in like storm troopers. "A lot of blood loss," "Square hit," "We don't want him going into shock." I'm strapped to a board and carried away. For a minute I think they have me on the grand board we used to roll in the piano. There is a surreal ride in an aid car, followed by the hubbub of an emergency room. I black out.

The next morning, when I open my eyes, I find my right hand encased in what resembles a monstrous white boxing glove. The nurses rib me. "Hate to think what the other guy looks like." My hand hurts like hell. I have a couple of broken fingers, fractured knuckles, and shredded nerves, the surgeon tells me. All is expected to heal — slowly. As loopy as the pain medications make me, one thing is perfectly clear. I will be seeking different work.

Yermy comes into my hospital room after the surgeon leaves. What I take for a look of contrition is him trying very hard not to crow when Veronica warily steps in behind him. Yermy is wearing the slacks and dress shirt from the previous evening's outfit. He doesn't need to tell me he never went home.

Veronica gives me a box of pastries from the Bon Ton. Yermy's gift to me is the truth. "Could be worse." He holds up his three-fingered hand. "Went to Chinatown for 'small' fireworks my first July First in Canada. Our version of your Independence Day. Loose fingers. Blew me off." His grin is a grimace, and I flash on the truism that a comedian goes back to something hurtful and makes it funny. Use the pain, don't let it use you.

"Blew me away," Veronica offers in a quiet, proprietary tone. Yermy's ardent smile at her blows *me* away. The man must be profoundly smitten to allow such correction.

⬦⬦⬦⬦⬦⬦⬦⬦⬦⬦⬦⬦⬦⬦⬦

After a week of inactivity, I have exhausted my computer skills, my left hand, my patience for TV, and the few people I can call. I have memorized Groucho's one-liners.

When I walk, out of boredom, to the corner coffee shop, I read every last notice on the wall of flyers. I learn that a bar in the neighborhood is starting an open mic comedy night. The thought of making a fool of myself in a bar seems less daunting after the double inoculations of ridicule at the synagogue fundraiser and excruciating pain from the hand accident. They happened, and I didn't die.

I could anesthetize myself with a few beers and regale the crowd with stories about working for a wacky Russian who desired the stage. Kept from his dream, he became, instead, a maestro of quips and barbs, a caretaker of aging parents, a conflicted Jew.

For all his clients, until Veronica, Yermy was like that third leg we slid underneath the piano when we were about to move it onto the grand board: necessary and, to his perpetual chagrin, rarely noticed. He found love moving a piano. Now that's funny, the kind of comedy that plumbs the disconnect between the ideal and what is. Joking about him would be all mixed up with how I feel about my estranged family, and my identity, and my great-grandfather's climb to fame and the slide to oblivion by the generations that followed.

I start practicing in front of my bathroom mirror.

Yeah, so I've just moved from Southern California—fleeing family—and it's a rainy fall day in Vancouver. Kind of romantic, really. I open a bottle of wine. Break up an old chair for kindling. Four months later, I'm an alcoholic with no furniture.

The crowd's laughter buoys me. I bob my head at them.

Of course, I wouldn't use my real name.

For Sale by Owner

Cantor Caroline moved away from her husband and next to Bruce. "May I hold your hand?"

Bruce could only nod and close his eyes, his voice useless. It was nice having her warm hand slide into his cold one. Another feeling besides pain.

Two large shovels stuck out of a mound of dirt next to Molly's open grave. The rabbi bypassed the shovels and with his hands scooped up wet soil, dropping it down onto the coffin. The sound made Bruce Stolover flinch. He had never heard it before. The large semi-circle of friends and family repeated the rabbi's action, but with shovels. It was raw enough shoveling in good clothes. No one wanted to get that dirty. They watched to see where the rabbi would wipe his hands.

Bruce's younger son, Jason, leaned against him, avoiding all eye contact. The older one, fifteen-year-old Josh, fidgeted with his hood, on again, off again, in the cold April drizzle. In Seattle it was attempting to be spring, with the usual chance of succeeding by summer. The cantor's daughter, Miri, shivered in a flimsy dress next to Josh, whom she had known since religious school kindergarten.

Molly's parents, sister, and brother stood apart. They had nothing against Bruce. He had given their Molly stability and the smoked glass kitchen cabinets for which she pined. They just weren't sure what to say and do around so many Jews.

Molly, a lukewarm Lutheran, had delegated to Bruce.

"These boys need some religion. Either you go find me a synagogue or I'll enroll them in Our Lady of the Lake," she had said, referring to the Catholic school down the street.

Caroline had started visiting regularly after Molly began chemotherapy. Their children had been closer friends than the two women, yet both mothers treasured those first sweet years that the kids were in Sunday school together. Josh, a robust little boy who woke up in the mornings wanting to hit things and fill the space, spent most play dates gazing rapturously at Miri. They all grew apart as they grew older. Caroline had two more children and Molly added animals to her household.

During one of Caroline's last visits, Molly had said she wanted to be buried in a small, old cemetery a few blocks from the house. Since she hadn't converted, she couldn't be buried in the large Jewish cemetery north of town and that was fine with her. "I want to be close to my boys. They can take the dogs out for a walk and come see me," Molly laughed with a croupy rattle.

Bruce inherited four animals from Molly. Hanukah was the dachshund she brought home to the boys during the holiday. She'd also rescued two kittens from a shelter and adopted the neighbor's beagle when the old lady died.

"First you don't let them in the house, then you don't let them on the furniture, finally, you put your foot down and don't let them on the bed," Bruce told Caroline and the others who came back with him to the house after Molly's burial. With a laugh that changed to a sob and back to a laugh, he shoved the beagle with his knee as it plopped its paws up for a better sniff of the overflowing kitchen counter. Josh and Jason, pacing around guests and furniture, watched the dachshund having a near-religious experience in the hall with someone's leather handbag. They forgot about wanting all the guests to leave and smiled at each other for the first time that day as the dog shredded the purse into slobbery particulate.

Caroline spent an hour at Bruce and Molly's home, nodding, making small, reassuring sounds, even humming, mostly listening to Bruce's memories. She looked at a photograph from Josh's Bar Mitzvah two years ago, a bloated Molly, full of cortisone, in her light blue suit and curly wig.

◇◇◇◇◇◇◇◇◇◇◇◇◇◇◇◇◇◇

When Jason's Bar Mitzvah came, Molly was six months gone.

Jason, the understated, overshadowed younger brother, had begun his speech and the congregation's surreptitious wiping gave way to audible sniffs.

The opening sentence alone, "I am so proud of my mother," sent congregants and guests fumbling for tissue. "She taught me a lot about really living each day. She spent her last weeks telling us what we were like as kids because she wanted us to remember the stories when she was gone. Kind of like Moses, in my Torah portion, at the end of his life."

"She told me that when I was four I asked her, 'Mom what happens to me when I die?'"

"She answered, 'Well honey, I'm not sure.'"

"And where was I before I was alive? I asked her."

"She said, 'I'm really not sure about that either.'"

"She said I looked at her with pity and said, 'It's okay, Mom, you can tell me!'"

The congregation had laughed gratefully. Bruce was awed at the way Jason made room for his dead mother on the *bimah*. She had died on Jason's watch. Curled in the armchair next to her bed, her beloved baby boy had opened his eyes that dawn to an unfamiliar, heart-stopping silence and he knew. He'd padded over to the living room couch and timidly shook his exhausted father's shoulder. "Dad, wake up," he'd said with teary relief. "Mom's gone."

"Thank God," Bruce whispered, "*haDan haEmet*," the True Judge. What else does one say at such a still, shattering moment?

It had been almost a year since Bruce had buried his wife and he was determined not to become a tragic figure. He kicked and stomped in karate class while his sons attended Tuesday night Hebrew school. He hired a house-keeper who was as efficient in keeping the place clean as in reminding him that Jesus could be his savior. He listed and sold houses regularly.

On those Tuesdays, the boys headed to the neighbor's, a street away, for dinner and a ride to religious school. Bruce went straight to karate after work and then to *shul* to pick up the kids for the homeward leg of the carpool. The physical workout and a relaxing shower meant a spring in his step, a bounce to his thinning red hair. He felt good, looked good, and liked catching a last tune or two in Cantor Caroline's Jewish music class for parents. She didn't seem to mind his late entry. The unmarried ladies in the class smiled at him. He smiled back, bantering softly with the cantor as she put away CDs and song sheets.

"I had a dream about us," Bruce revealed to her one week as the last parent left. "It was somewhere during the Holocaust with lots of smoke and fighting."

"How did we do?" Caroline asked lightly, pushing the sheet music into a stack.

"Oh, we survived. In fact, we more than just survived."

She looked straight at him.

"It was war time," he explained with a suggestive smile.

Bruce wondered if Caroline ever dreamed about him. Her blush made him wonder if he could tell something about her she preferred to keep secret.

He wanted to reassure her he was sensitive and evolved and looking for a woman, but hardly psychic, or into married women. He could understand that even the most secure, loving, middle-aged spouses ask, *what if?*, from time to time. He didn't see himself crossing that social line with Cantor Caroline. Dream the dream forward, his therapist had told him just that week, and the risks reveal themselves.

The next week, Bruce got to class a little earlier. His snug jeans and tight shirt showed off his muscles. The unmarried ladies watched his well-defined buttocks. Now that he was working out, his belt was too long and dangled in front of his zipper, and he liked that. Caroline looked him over discreetly and continued discussing the origins of a song.

"How's the running going?" he asked her after class. He knew she was training for a long-distance run.

"I'm up to fourteen miles." Caroline ducked his gaze, but pulled her waistband out exultantly. "And I'm down to a size 10! I'm in better shape now than when I was in college. Takes some of the angst out of advancing gray hair and wrinkles!"

Stepping close to her, Bruce whipped off his glasses and closed his eyes. For one startling moment, it seemed he meant to kiss her.

"Look at this stuff above my eyes," he ordered. She strained to see what could be wrong.

"The skin," Bruce said, exasperated. "It's rolling down over my eyes like window shades." Caroline laughed.

"We should go have a glass of wine sometime," he suggested.

"Yes, that would be nice," she murmured. "I know such an invitation would be appreciated even more by the single moms in the class."

Bruce gave a small snort, "I'm not interested in people who have designs on me."

He enjoyed the "Is that so?" challenge of Caroline's arched eyebrows.

◇◇◇◇◇◇◇◇◇◇◇◇◇◇◇◇◇◇

Bruce climbed upstairs with a young couple during a Sunday afternoon open house. He swung a glass door open. "This is the master bedroom. Some view." He watched the wife look at the giant bed, out to the Sound, and over to her husband. She smiled broadly. The owner, who had left town for a better job, had agreed with Bruce that the house would sell more quickly with the high-end furnishings still in it.

The wife turned to Bruce. "We'll be right down. Can you give us a few minutes?"

He walked out of the bedroom and down the stairs. It had worked before, he hummed to himself. It should work again. Before the day was out, he would have an offer to give his client.

He waited on a spotless, white leather couch for the young couple and thought about his place. Bruce did not want to sleep with a woman in his house. The boys were always around, with those stupid, barking dogs and regal cats. It was Molly's house, anyway. How could he have sex with anyone else in the house she had found and furnished? They had brought two sons home to it. She had breathed her last in it. Twenty-two years under the same roof with the same take-no-shit woman. He had to respect that, and, not sure why, he wanted the cantor to know that too.

The next Tuesday, he was back in Caroline's music class, in need of a confidant.

Bruce glanced around the empty classroom. "Every marriage has its issues."

Caroline looked away while Bruce took a deep breath.

"Molly and I became close friends that last year, closer than we had ever been in all the years of our marriage. She taught me how to cook, how to take care of the boys, what needed to be done around the house."

Bruce pushed up his glasses and wiped his eyes.

"I miss her most when we should be celebrating as a family. This is kind of embarrassing, but the afternoon Josh graduated from middle school, I went up to the cemetery and sat down next to her and finished off a six pack."

◇◇◇◇◇◇◇◇◇◇◇◇◇◇◇◇◇◇◇◇◇

It was April again. Bruce and the boys picked a pink granite headstone for Molly and set a date to mark the anniversary.

"What exactly do you do at an unveiling?" Bruce asked Caroline at the end of a music class.

"You use songs and prayers and testimonials. You've lived without her for a year, Bruce. You're a different person. An unveiling confirms that. Some Jews simply pull off a tombstone's gauze cover," Caroline said.

"Is it okay to sing a Beatles' song?" he asked.

She smiled and got her guitar.

"There are places I remember…." Her voice retreated when she saw Bruce's quivering lips. She lowered her eyes.

"You loved her, too," he whispered.

As at Molly's burial, the weather at the unveiling was cold and gray. Bruce asked the handful of friends if they had anything to say. One gruff, gray-bearded man clapped an arm around Bruce's shoulder. "Molly's left her boys in good hands." A woman placed a bouquet of tulips next to the little headstone.

Bruce nodded at Caroline, and in a breathy, constricted voice, hardly her own, she got through the song, "… in my-y-y-y-y life, I loved you more."

Finally, in Hebrew, she and Bruce chanted the ancient words of the *Kaddish.*

"It's an expression of thanks for the power of memory, more than a lament for a loss," Caroline announced. The others watched curiously. This time non-Jews outnumbered Jews. "*Yitgadal v'yitkadash sh'mei raba*"…Let the glory of God be extolled, let God's great name be hallowed.

"It's time for the birds." Bruce motioned to a woman standing next to a large white box.

"These are homing pigeons," the woman said, holding up one white bird. "They'll fly around a few times to get their bearings and then head back to the roost."

Clumsy in the first seconds of their release, the birds swerved and tumbled, dodging the tall Douglas firs that had been growing long before the land was cleared for a cemetery. All those assembled lifted pensive faces into the mist and watched the birds rise in a frenzied circle.

◇◇◇◇◇◇◇◇◇◇◇◇◇◇◇◇◇

The following week, Bruce again lingered after music class. Caroline congratulated him on a beautiful unveiling ceremony. She pulled on a raincoat and they walked out to her car.

"The rabbi's been after us to move to the neighborhood," she said. "I'd love to be able to walk home after class or on Shabbat."

And there it was, a date made to see houses.

That morning, Bruce brushed his teeth and flossed. He put on his tailored, blue power-sales dress shirt and the brown loafers with tassels. He drove by two houses he planned to show her and put bottles of champagne in the refrigerators before driving to her house.

She was waiting on the front steps. With black, curly hair and almond-shaped green eyes, the cantor looked so different from Molly. Molly had been a wispy blonde, simple and good. What you saw with Molly was pretty much what you got. With other women, you could never be sure, though.

Two weeks after Molly had died, Josh, poring over a family photo album, had tearfully looked up at Bruce.

"Dad, I don't want you dating anyone."

Bruce had thought carefully before answering, unsure of the source of this demand.

"Josh, your mother and I were together for twenty-two years and some years were better than others. There were even times when we thought about separating, before she got sick."

"Oh, yeah, I know," Josh came back in the puncturing tone of fifteen-year-old deflationists. "She showed us where Jason and I were going to live with her."

"You just want to hurt me as bad as you're hurting," Bruce snarled, surprised.

Bruce felt that same instant upwelling of emotion at the sound of the key in the lockbox of the first house. *Make it happen*, he willed, ushering in Caroline. They wandered from room to room on the lower floor, every word and look charged with the unspoken question, *when?* In the master bedroom she gazed out the window long enough for him to come up behind her. He noticed goose bumps on the back of her neck and he felt sure he saw a tiny shiver crawl down her back.

An inch from her ear, Bruce whispered, "Only if you want to."

Slowly, her eyes turned first, then her nose and face. Her body appeared to be fighting with itself — turn around, don't turn around. She came to face him.

"I wouldn't dream of making such a big decision unless, unless I wanted to," she faltered.

Bruce's stomach curled in anticipation and he felt the right stirrings in the right place. Her breaths came in tiny, inaudible pants.

Caroline grasped the bedpost for support and directed her next words to the floor. "It's one thing to enact a fantasy in the confines of my brain and quite another to have a living, breathing person ready to misbehave with me in a stranger's house," she conceded with a gasp. "I am sorry. I've let things go too far."

For an eternal moment Bruce floundered, then brightened, "I'll take that as a counteroffer?" Maybe he could still sell her a house.

In the end, Caroline's husband stumbled on the perfect place, for sale by owner, just three blocks from *shul.* Caroline suggested Bruce lead them through the negotiations. He was happy to oblige.

The evening the final papers were to be signed, Bruce retrieved the two bottles of unopened champagne, one to be presented to Caroline and her husband at closing, the other for a date in the cemetery. Why not? His sons were at a baseball game.

Bruce shook hands with Caroline and her husband and put the signed documents in his briefcase. The three of them walked down the dark driveway to Bruce's car and shook again before Caroline and her husband, hand-in-hand, strolled gleefully back to take another look at their new home.

Bruce leaned against his car and watched the sky for a long time. Black holes, rimmed in weak yellow, bore through the backlit clouds, implying a moon. A star break, he hoped. He drove to the cemetery and parked, taking time to watch the fluid night sky before reaching for the champagne bottle and uncorking it. There were no street lamps around the cemetery and certainly none in it. He leaned against his car and took a short fizzy swig, noticing the shadow of his upheld arm on the hood of the car. The moon had broken free of its cloudy captors, providing him with enough light to find his way to Molly.

Off the Cusp

Tivon's eyes glistened like red, hard-boiled eggs, the result of his three-day trek from Kenya to Bellingham, a blur of troubled sleep, unyielding armrests, and thick-headed customs agents. He kept rolling his eyes and rubbing them with long fingers. The color of eggplant, Tivon was one of four exchange students from Africa who would be studying in my father's lab at Western Washington College in 1966. I was starting a new school too, as a freshman in high school.

Tivon's bag of toiletries had disappeared en route. Over lunch, my parents, Miriam and Alan, my younger sister, Lisa, and I helped him make a replacement list.

"My comb is in that lost bag." Tivon closed his eyes, thumb and middle finger massaging the wide bridge of his nose.

"In the meantime, you could use one of these," Daddy said earnestly, staring at his fork.

My mother and I yelped. She in disgust, I in delight. I giggled at the thought of Tivon twirling his kinky hair like spaghetti with one of our fancy dinner forks.

My father was ready to construct the wide-toothed comb Tivon described. My mother insisted we look in the drugstore downtown. Or, maybe the local barber knew where to get one, she said.

Lisa went off to play with the neighbor girls and the rest of us got in the car. I sat in back with the exhausted Tivon, whose head, I feared, would land in my lap the way it lolled around as we drove.

My parents had instructed Lisa and me to be kind to Tivon, far from his African homeland. I didn't know he would be a handsome young man, palms the translucent pink of my Florida conch shell. My multi-lingual father was intrigued with Tivon's name, for in Hebrew it meant, "a student of nature."

"He's a natural," Daddy had reiterated until our groans stopped him. "I must remember to ask him how he came by such a name."

We parked and I poked Tivon awake, pointing to the hypnotic red, white, and blue spiral of the barber pole.

The first thing I saw in the barbershop was a giant glass jar filled with hundreds of lollipops. The colors reminded me of amphibians in my father's slide shows: blue frogs of South America, yellow wrasses off Cuba's coasts. Color as warning. Living with my father meant knowing terms like aposematic coloration, used throughout the animal kingdom to advertise poison or other dangerous defensive strategies. The acid-green lollipops looked appealing.

When we walked in the shop, all conversation stopped. Two seated men stared at Tivon over their *Hunting and Fishing* magazines. The barber turned his back to us and continued cutting hair.

"I don't want anything that black in my shop. Why'd he bring that nigger in here?" The barber seemed stumped by my father's imprudence.

My mother's eyes opened impossibly wide, her eyebrows practically lifting off her face. Tivon stood, watchful, smile gone, looking from me to my parents.

I imagined my father intoning to the barber, *Some species use bright coloration to advertise to their predators that they are unpalatable.*

I studied Tivon's purple-black skin. Would he blush at the barber's verbal attack? My father once told me that even the great Darwin wondered if people with dark skin blush. With a mental snigger I remembered Darwin's second question, "And especially how low down the body does the blush extend?"

"I guess they're busy," Daddy said. He jerked the front door open so that Tivon, my mother, and I were sucked out the door and onto the sidewalk after him as if by a giant wave of receding water. I fingered the lollipop in my pocket in pleased revenge.

Outside, my mother grimaced. "Oh, Alan, even here?" She turned away so Tivon could not see her brimming eyes.

I knew what she was talking about. Two years ago, when we still lived in New Jersey, and Mississippi was the challenge word on our geography spelling test, James Chaney, Andrew Goodman, and Michael Schwerner were killed while investigating a church fire and registering black voters. Mother had grown up next door to Schwerner's family in New York. She'd cried for days when the young men's beaten bodies were found that Freedom Summer of 1964. She cried when my father called her about landing the job as department head in Bellingham, Washington. Is that near D.C.?, the relatives asked.

Lisa and I had made our mother little get-well cards, brought her dandelions and wild daisies. It frightened us to see our sniffling mother lying down fully dressed, not bothering to take off her heels and nylons, wet washcloth across her forehead.

This afternoon, as Tivon napped, I tried out the word that sounded like a slap.

Nigger.

I said it in front of the bathroom mirror and then to impress my sister.

"Tivon got called a nigger today."

Lisa said nothing. She was only eight.

"It's a bad word and the barber said it in front of all of us." I used my gravest tones.

She grasped that something VERY SERIOUS had happened. "Did Tivon cry?"

"He's a college student," I huffed. "He was so brave."

I marched into the kitchen.

"I want to show Tivon *my* America," I told my mother.

"He can see *your* America tomorrow," my mother countered. "Go outside and take Lisa with you and be quiet. The poor man hasn't slept in days."

The front screen slammed four or five times an hour as I kept checking to see if Tivon was up yet. My exasperated mother grabbed my shoulders and pushed me out the door, "Stay out."

I wanted to show Tivon everything. It was all nearly as new to me as it was to him: the tire swing at the end of the pebbly road we shared with five other families, my route under the power lines to Paul Revere High School, our neighbor's horses.

From our tree house, built by the previous owner, you could see the mountains, pure and incisive, wearing their first shawl of snow.

"He's probably never seen snow," I said to Lisa. With a sharp intake of breath, I decided I would be the one to show him. Hi, I'm Rae Ann Shifren, America's favorite teenage guide. Our next stop? Let's take Tivon to his first Dairy Dell. I imagined Lisa and I holding our breath as he wrestled with that monumental decision. Dip the swirl of soft vanilla ice cream in the chocolate or in the peppermint vat?

Lisa and I wandered over to our neighbor's house, where a late harvest of their small apple orchard was underway. Kids ducked and pitched rotten apples and got yelled at when a mushy missile landed too close to a grown-up. Caramel-colored juice poured from the cider press. Women hurried out with steaming, sterilized bottles. We kids drank glass after frothy glass. The juice smelled like autumn sky, tasted of leaf piles and cinnamon, sweet and earthy.

Dusk's brittle cold overtook a crisp afternoon. Our apple battles wound down, throws reduced to aimless wobbles as fingers stiffened and hands went numb.

When Lisa and I came back to the house, Tivon was awake. My mother was trying to feed him again.

Cheese tasted like soap to him. Jello made him gag. Junket was worse. For the second time, Tivon made a list: potatoes, cabbage, corn, and lamb. He looked through my mother's spice rack, sniffing at jars until he found the right smells, curry and cumin.

"Tomorrow I cook," he announced.

From the end of the driveway the next day, I sniffed something exotic. School worries vanished. Instead, my mind conjured up tawny lions, spice bazaars, trickling water in shimmering deserts. I banged open the front door and dropped my satchel.

"What is that smell?" I yelled.

Tivon motioned to a big pot on the stove and aimed a wooden spoon at me. He blew on a cube of lamb he had fished out, setting it on my tongue as if it were a diamond. I could tell from my mother's slight frown that she wasn't sure if his feeding me was quite proper.

"It's what we make in my village," Tivon said with a proud smile, adding a phrase in another language that left my mother, sister, and I blinking vacantly.

"We'll call it Lamb Macharia," my mother chirped. "After you, Tivon Macharia," she repeated, in case he hadn't understood.

A dish was born, my palate expanded, and Tivon's standing heightened. A man who could cook! The stew needed to simmer, my chance to show him the neighborhood.

"Be back in half an hour," Mother called after us.

I strolled with Tivon past waving grass pastures and fence posts pitted from trigger-happy boys. Having never walked alone nor chatted with a young man in such a grown-up manner, I felt mature and socially desirable, a welcome sensation from having been pigeon-holed by my classmates as that *brainy new girl from back East.*

For me, life in Bellingham wasn't so bad, I told Tivon. It was my mother who missed her family in the urban cities of the East.

Tivon said he had missed his family, too, when he boarded at a school in Nairobi. On the weekends, he'd hitched a ride or walked home. His four older sisters lived near his parents in his village. His younger brother still lived at home.

"My mother taught my sisters to cook. They would slap my hands when I tried to help, but I learned anyway," he laughed.

"My sisters all have husbands and they can thank me for teaching them how to raise a little boy. They cried when I left. They said, 'We are sending away our first son.'"

Tivon inclined his head at me. "In Kenya, girls your age are already married and some have babies."

At fourteen! Astounding news. "Don't they have to go to school?"

Tivon gave a sarcastic laugh. "You don't know what a blessing it is that you are allowed to go to school. What say I wait until you graduate, and then we can marry and have chocolate milk children?"

My queasiness with this familiarity must have shown, because Tivon threw back his head and laughed for real.

"You Americans are all so serious." His pink palm gently yanked my ponytail. In my head, I heard my father lecturing: *When grabbed by a predator, salamanders and lizards make use of a unique breakaway tail. The animal releases its tail and runs away. The tail eventually grows back.*

I heard the raspy station wagon long before I saw it, and felt a nip of nervousness. It was Danny Dishman, our neighbor, and three other boys coming home from football practice.

"Yoo hoo, Rae Ann, who's your new boyfriend?" Danny yelled, stopping the car. He leaned forward for a good look. An icy sword of embarrassment ran through me. The boy in the front seat, Stewart Randolph, made a lewd gesture.

"Meet Tivon, from Kenya, Africa," I entreated them.

Danny floored the gas pedal and peeled away, scattering pebbles and insecurity. In my nascent teenage world of vacillating allegiances, Tivon went from cool diversion to unwanted company. We needed to go back anyway. I put more space between him and me, even walked a step ahead.

At the familiar raspy sound, I turned around and saw Danny and Stewart returning. He pulled the car over to block our way. The two boys got out.

Stewart had a gun. This did not immediately register to me as dangerous. It seemed like everybody's father had guns out here. They all hunted deer or shot clay pigeons. In the short time we had been in Bellingham some kid, playing with his father's guns, had accidentally shot himself and a friend.

When I looked at Tivon's face, I realized this might be different.

"They got guns like this in Kenya?" drawled Stewart, only he said Keeenyah, holding up what looked like a hunting rifle. What did I know from guns? My father was head of the biology department and a Jew. No guns in our house.

Danny's smirk made me aware of my bladder. Stewart looked through the rifle's scope and pointed it over Tivon's shoulder, whipped it down and shot at the pavement near our feet. I mightily squeezed the muscles of my pelvic floor to avoid wetting myself.

Stewart shot at the pavement again, white gravel powder arcing towards the ditch. "What are you doing?" I screamed.

"Jump higher, higher, pants on fire, big black crow on the telephone wire," Danny called out. Stewart laughed, all teeth and long neck. Like a raucous raven jockeying for a share in a road kill, I thought. I was desperate for a car to come by.

Then came a sound that turned my body into one giant goose bump. A moan and a shriek at the same time, it was coming from Tivon's throat, only it didn't seem human. Stewart lowered his rifle, suspicious. Danny stepped back.

Tivon's eyes were closed and his head back, his mouth puckered into a tight o. He was gulping in air through reared-back nostrils, and the sound never stopped.

"What the hell is that?" Stewart seemed hypnotized. No one moved, could move. We were statuary at the side of the road, as if a photographer, driving by at that moment, insisted we hold a pose while he reloaded his camera. Snap. Snap.

Honk.

The best sound in the world, the dippy horn on my mother's turquoise Plymouth. She pulled over and, as she got out, Stewart eased the gun into Danny's car through an open back window.

"Hi, boys." My mother gave them a perfunctory wave before turning to me.

"Rae Ann, I don't appreciate you out here socializing when the rest of us at home are waiting on dinner. I told you to be back in thirty minutes. Tivon, please get in the front."

At dinner I kept glancing at Tivon, waiting for him to bring up our frightening encounter. He shook his head slightly when he caught my look and put a long finger against his lips.

The Lamb Macharia was, well, different. Lisa and I were used to meatloaf with catsup. Halfway through dinner my father rose and came back with something he had made. It looked like a tiny pitchfork, a new comb for Tivon.

I waited to get Tivon alone, approaching him the minute my mother headed upstairs to put Lisa to bed. Mother always fell asleep reading to Lisa.

"What was that sound you made in front of the boys?"

"A hunter makes this when he surprises prey. It makes the animal stop for a moment, and in that instant the other hunters shoot it."

"How did you keep doing it for so long?"

Tivon didn't know how to say it in English. I grabbed his hand and led him into the living room where my father sat screened behind a newspaper. I was dying to tell Daddy what had happened, even as I knew Tivon was not.

"Circular breathing," my father explained. "Why was Tivon doing this? Who were these boys you were visiting with, Rae Ann?" My father was using his "a-stiff-prick-has-no-conscience" tone I recognized from recent birds-and-bees conversations.

My tears ambushed me. I croaked out the story, Daddy's face grew still and stony at my mention of the gun. He nodded when I described Tivon's response.

"Of course, secondary defense," Daddy said. I knew an explanation was coming. "Startle or intimidation displays during an encounter with an enemy increase the chance of escape and survival."

"As opposed to primary defense," he continued, giving me his stern professor look. "That prevents an encounter with an enemy or predator."

Daddy told me to go to bed. In the morning he would call Danny's father. My heart hung suspended, impending social banishment rolling down on my head.

"Why do you have to call?" I hurled at him.

I raced upstairs, locked my bedroom door, and rolled underneath my bed. My parents did not know that the heating duct under my bed was a perfect conduit for conversations going on in the living room. Already I had learned much with my ear jammed against the grate.

I heard my father apologize to Tivon for the racist behavior he had encountered during his first days in Bellingham. Tivon tried to joke it off, saying the way white people treat black people in America is the way some black people treat each other in Africa.

They started talking biology. I heard them opening bottles. Tivon loved cold beer. "Nothing better on the hottest days in Kenya," he said.

"Once again, driving home the necessity for contrary conditions," responded my father with a rueful chuckle.

A bottle clunked down on the coffee table, followed by my father's voice. "Without good, there would be no evil. Without sizzling heat, would cold beer taste so good?" I could hear Tivon chuckle. Their voices grew mumbly, their laughter easier.

When Lisa and I came down for breakfast, the men had left to register Tivon for classes and to get him moved into the campus dorms. Tivon might have left a note for me, I thought. My mother was hurt too. Tivon had declined her offer of Friday night Shabbat dinner.

"He'll change his mind after a few days on cafeteria food," Mother predicted, heading into the guest room. She came back with her nose wrinkled and an armful of linens.

"He peed in the bed," she said, aghast. "And he must have been too embarrassed to tell me."

"Tivon and Daddy were drinking beers last night and he probably had too much," I said without thinking.

"How do you know?" she and Lisa asked at the same time.

Bluffing and evasion rank among the more effective defenses against predators. This behavior is called distraction display.

"Mother," I paused, searching. "What color babies do a white person and a black person make?"

"What? Probably tan."

"Would the children have kinky hair?"

"I imagine."

Mother frowned, likely struggling to remember what we had been talking about before my questions.

Looking back, I now know that what I felt was jilted. Granted, I wouldn't have known to have used that word then. My teenaged heart felt toyed with.

Like a rejected child, I decided I didn't want any chocolate milk babies, probably couldn't find combs for them anyway, and if the guy was going to wet the bed every time he had a few beers he was going to wait for me forever. I wouldn't wait even ten minutes for him. I may even have stamped a foot.

"I don't need that nigger in my life."

Mother rounded on me.

"We don't use words like that in our house. He is a black man or a Negro or Tivon. I will not tolerate racial slurs from you."

I knew I had transgressed. In utter confusion over the emotional upwelling Tivon's stay had caused, I could only shrug at her before putting on my coat. I made a show of checking the pockets for gloves. "Fall in the Northwest can be surprisingly cold," I simpered.

"You've let me down, Rae Ann."

"He let me down."

Lisa and I walked down the driveway blowing clouds of steam at each other, pretending to be dragons. The morning draped itself around us like pink tulle. Stray rays of sun glinted off the bellies of doves, turning them into flying apricot gems. I waved good-bye to Lisa at her elementary school and joined the sleepy teenagers at the high school bus stop a few streets over.

To the north, an Orangeade sky colored the mountains. Tons of snow, I willed, leaning my forehead against the cool bus window. Tivon wouldn't last one of the Northwest's well-known blizzards.

I, on the other hand, would sip marshmallow-festooned cocoa and listen to my father dictate a paper to my mother, a much more competent typist than any secretary, Daddy always declared. As snow piled up past our windows, the dining room would echo with the clicking typewriter and the fire's crackle. Lisa would be asleep with her blankie on the couch. I'd snuggle into my sleeping bag by the fire and read, with no one outside my world to complicate things.

◇◇◇◇◇◇◇◇◇◇◇◇◇◇◇◇◇◇

The snow started the night of the homecoming football game. Danny Dishman asked me to the dance and I reluctantly said yes, wondering if it wasn't some sadistic bargain between Danny and my father to keep law enforcement from becoming aware of the "incident." During the first quarter a few flakes salted our hair. By the third quarter the snow was getting far more attention than the action on the field. The football players, blowing into their hands to keep warm, slipped and spun out of control as the crowd dwindled. The dance was cancelled. On the slow drive back home, I pictured Tivon's dark face turned up to the white sky, snowflakes piling up on his black, black lashes. A couple days of sitting cross-legged on my bedroom floor, extracting terrible chords on an out-of-tune guitar did the trick. I rose up — with Tivon behind me. My mother nudged my father. "She's done sitting *shivah*."

A few weeks later when I thought to ask about Tivon, the look my mother shot my father showed me they were worried about him. A subsequent late-night exchange I heard, via the heating duct, confirmed this. Tivon was not applying himself, Daddy told my mother. Tivon was failing a biochemistry class, and two other professors had asked my father to set up tutoring for Tivon.

"You gave him the chance. That's a gift," my mother soothed.

During Thanksgiving vacation I tromped through a white, silent campus with my father, a rare time when he let me feed the lab animals. A descending, concrete sky, from which snow would fall in punishing amounts that winter, spit tiny flakes at us.

A few students materialized, like bundled phantoms, for a snowball fight. Worried that one might be Tivon, I looked straight ahead and slunk down beside my father. The keen observer of animal behavior noticed.

"Tivon went home with his roommate over vacation," Daddy said with an uncharacteristic sigh. "He's become quite attentive to his roommate's sister."

I hung back a petulant moment to scoop up a powdery ball of snow. I gave it a half-hearted toss in my father's direction.

When he turned to answer my volley with a hoot and a perfectly aimed throw, Daddy was a merry college student himself — an image so wonderful, so new, I forgot to dodge and the snowball clipped my chin. "Gotcha!" he razzed, and I burst into tears.

I ran up behind my father and wrapped my arms around his solid middle. I'll never know how he knew to slide me around to his front and silently hold me as I cried out my ambivalence over our new lives. Fathers in the Sixties didn't usually do that, certainly. I believe it was in that moment of simple homage to a man who seemed to have all the answers, that I was eased off the cusp between childhood and fledging adult empathy.

In his face I suddenly had seen a youth I wished I had known, a youth who could well have pulled a ponytail or two, whose unfiltered boyish banter might have emboldened a young girl's heart. In silence we walked glove-in-glove to the science building, the rhythmic crunch of our footsteps like a vocabulary of passage.

Triage

The end-of-June deluge hurt Tibor's eyes. Violin cases lay everywhere. Guitars with broken necks and saxes with odious dents languished on counters. A particularly sickening note, "Stepped On," was taped to the outside of a cello case. He would have to work up to opening that one.

There used to be a brass man and a woodwind man working side-by-side with Tibor, the string man. After they retired, Seattle School District's instrument repair department became Tibor. Budget shortfalls, the higher-ups told him. Tibor had complained mightily. A few papers were shuffled. The higher-ups dangled a summer intern in front of him each year.

I'll never get it all done by September, Tibor had whined. Give me a craftsman, not someone I gotta teach. It'll take forever.

Still, for the past five years, he had single-handedly crossed the Labor Day Weekend finish line with everything restrung, reglued, repadded, polished and cleaned — only to have the little darlings spend the school year destroying all his good work.

Tibor, tiring and sixty-two, was disinclined to mention the tremors in his hands and his fatigue from straining over the bench, especially with the big basses. This summer he had reluctantly accepted help from an interplanetary program, or some such *mishegas*, such hooey.

"Evergreen's Interdisciplinary Studies Program has successfully placed its students around the world," the gray-haired school district administrator informed him. "We're thrilled to have Chia working with you this summer." In Tibor's opinion, Evergreen, about an hour south of Seattle, was one of those loony little liberal arts colleges that attracted directionless navel gazers.

Today, the administrator stepped over flute cases and past the mountainous workshop counters to look out the large windows. "I had no idea you had such a great view up here." A thousand tiny suns winked off the waves in Elliott Bay.

Tibor looked at the person waiting by the door. Man or woman? The corduroy pants, the striped short-sleeved shirt, and the work boots certainly could have been worn by a man. The close-cropped blue hair and the tiny earstuds could belong to a woman. Those faint mounds might be breasts.

His long-dead father's voice drifted through Tibor's mind: *Az di bobe volt gehat a bord, volt zi geven a zayde*, if the grandmother had a beard, she would be a grandfather. Tibor liked the racier version, *Az di bobe volt gehat baytzim, volt zi geven a zayde*, if the grandmother had balls....

The person standing by the door took Tibor's faint, faraway smile for an invitation. Hand extended, he or she walked into Tibor's sunny workshop, a universe of floating dust motes.

Tibor stared at the hand and did not put out his own. Garish colors were etched into the skin around the person's right wrist. The five black numbers tattooed into the inside of his or her forearm startled Tibor the most.

"What kind of a statement is this?" he snarled. Young people and their insanities: desecrating tattoos, bizarre hair, weird lifestyles.

"It honors the memory of my grandfather, who was in a concentration camp," Chia said, in a woman's voice.

"You'd do better by him by finding a husband and naming your children in your grandfather's honor."

The school district administrator turned back from the window. "Now, now, Tibor, you're living up to your reputation as a character," she reproved. "I have a few papers." She extended her pen and pointed to the lines where she wanted him to sign.

"I'll want to read these first."

"Then I'll come back." The administrator sighed grandly, ushering Chia towards the door. "I want to show Chia around the building. Oh..." The administrator came close to Tibor. "Remember, the new District policy requires that when working with a student, doors need to remain open," she said in a low voice. Tibor rolled his eyes. *Oy.*

◇◇◇◇◇◇◇◇◇◇◇◇◇◇◇◇◇◇◇

For the past year, Tibor had dutifully hauled himself up the stairs leading to the third floor repair shop. He used the elevator only for bringing up basses and tubas. The climb, which had started out as a practical nod to his doctor's infernal lectures about getting exercise, had become something of a ritual ascent after his grandsons' visit.

Eli and the other little boy, Ezra, had bounced up the steps in front of Tibor, waiting for him to open the heavy door to the third floor. When Tibor pulled the door back, dazzling sunshine from the workshop's big windows had made everything blindingly white. Apparently, to Eli's eyes, the cellos and basses, outlined by the shivery light, looked like welcoming angels.

"*Papoo*, we're in instrument heaven," the little boy had shouted, awestruck, arms flung wide.

The boys ran past the practice rooms and climbed up on the counter to look out.

"Off, off." Tibor curled his arms around the boys and swept them down. He'd handed out sticks, and the three of them had carried a drum kit into one of the practice rooms.

"Have at it," he chuckled.

Tibor had vaguely thought he would be called *zayde*, grandfather, someday. By marrying Fortuna Calvo, he instead had been swept into the world and words of Seattle's Sephardic community. A mixed marriage, he always said with amusement. Tibor learned to eat bischochos and grape leaves stuffed with currants and rice. The melodies at Sephardic Bikur Holim synagogue were like Mediterranean love songs, luscious compared to the expeditious chants he'd learned from his Hungarian father.

Tibor's son had married a girl whose family came from the Isle of Rhodes. The young couple produced two chocolate-eyed grandsons for *Papoo* Tibor and *Nona* Fortuna, and a third grandchild was on the way, *mashallah, mashallah*.

Though he missed having someone with whom to laugh at naughty Yiddish proverbs, Tibor had no complaints really. None of the Sephardic people his parents' age hid dark blue numbers under long-sleeved shirts.

◇◇◇◇◇◇◇◇◇◇◇◇◇◇◇◇◇◇◇

While the viola was not his favorite member of the string family, when the new one came in with the rest of the year-end instruments, Tibor immediately appreciated its worth. To him, a viola was like a beautiful woman with a never-ending cold. This one, a wide-hipped wench with a sound like a nagging goose, was expertly made. He ran his fingers up the fingerboard and over the scroll.

"Look," he said to Chia, pointing out a razor-thin line just below the back of the scroll. "Could go back to Beethoven's time. That's when they started elongating the necks to give them more notes. They kept the original scrolls and bodies, and glued on new necks and fingerboards."

Chia's eyes widened. "My violin has the same cut. You mean it could be over 200 years old?"

"Maybe. Bring it in sometime. I'd like to see it."

Chia's fingers caressed the viola's inlaid border. "It's got to be worth a lot."

Tibor kept his estimate to himself. It was easily a $10,000 instrument, and what-in-hell was it doing in their hands? Some family must have given it to a school's string program without knowing what they had. He would make inquiries among the symphony players and look for a buyer. No way was he going to send this blowzy beauty back out into the schools. He shooed Chia away.

"All those need strings." He pointed to a row of violin cases.

"My other grandfather played viola. In New York, in a symphony."

"Anybody play it now?'

"I don't know what happened to it."

"Never thought to ask?"

"We're a pretty estranged family—Jewish, Latina, Irish."

Tibor gave a small, noncommittal grunt. His job was to repair instruments, not relationships.

"Strings," he ordered, jerking his thumb in the direction of the violins.

A few days later, near the top steps to the third floor, Tibor heard indistinct string music. Must have left the radio on yesterday, he thought. The music grew louder as he opened the third floor door and approached the practice rooms. He peeked through a small window and saw Chia and an auburn-haired girl, backs to the door, attentive to the sheet music on their stands. Mozart's Sinfonia Concertante for violin and viola, Tibor registered.

He watched the girls sway and whip the pages over, lifting up slightly from their chairs, urgent sensuality to their movements. A rare flush of embarrassment spread up his neck and face and made him turn away. Two girls playing a duet, two instruments making love, or, the other way around. The auburn-haired girl was good. In her hands the usual honk of the viola was honey.

Tibor walked into the opened shop area. Chia must have gotten one of the custodians to unlock the place early. The sight of the violist reminded him that he wanted to stop by Lou Carrabba's strings store and have the new viola appraised.

He surveyed the shelves, flustered and then concerned. Finally, he realized the auburn-haired girl was playing it.

He rapped on the practice room door and tugged it open.

"What's going on here?" He didn't care how nasty he sounded.

Chia whirled around, violin sliding off her skinny shoulder.

"Oh, I'm sorry. This is my partner, Nurit. I told her about the viola and we thought we'd try it out."

Partner? Business partner? Stand partner? Tibor struggled momentarily with Chia's meaning, while taking in Nurit's untold cinnamon freckles. Freckles even on her lips. Nurit had all the curves Chia did not. A big round bottom and breasts that put the mamma in mammary, Tibor noted with interest. Nurit looked like a viola. He had heard of people looking like their dogs, but like their instruments?

"You are an intern here, Chia," Tibor snapped. "You need my permission before you let anyone touch these instruments, especially that one." He held out his hands for the viola. Nurit glanced sideways at Chia before giving Tibor the instrument and bow.

"She knows what she's doing," Chia said quietly.

Nurit stayed Tibor's left arm as he bent down for the viola case. "Might we rehearse here? Under your supervision, of course." No sign of guilt or remorse for her forward actions, and she was challenging him to be a gentleman. Her slow, accented English disarmed him. He knew that accent.

"*Ihr redt Yiddish?*" he asked.

"*Yo, ikh red Yiddish, Hebraish, un Ungarish.*"

Chia looked put out. "What?"

Tibor made an "akkkhhh" sound from the back of his throat. "Your friend and I speak the same languages." He softened. "You can only use the viola when I am here. And today I need her." He walked regally into the workshop, instrument under his arm, fully expecting a response.

"Tomorrow then?" Nurit called.

"I'll let Chia know." Tibor wasn't going to make it easy. He put the viola in its case and began looking for Carrabba's number. He heard the girls whispering. Chia came into the workshop alone. "Where should I start?" she asked, polite and sunny, clearly having been coached.

Carrabba confirmed what Tibor suspected. The viola was well made and worth a lot. It would be easy to find a buyer. Did Tibor want him to make some calls?

Tibor shook his head and snapped the case shut. Funny, he didn't want to let it out of his hands just yet. Nurit could use it over the summer, he decided. She had been accepted to the Eastman School of Music in the fall. He'd get back with Carrabba at summer's end.

Tibor enjoyed listening to the girls' morning duets. He waited for chats in Yiddish with Nurit when she returned the viola to him. She was Israeli, of Hungarian parentage. His eyes stung unexpectedly when one day she coyly teased him with Hungarian nursery rhymes. "*Oz ein apukam egy oyan hiresh boholthz volt…*My father was such a famous clown…" She flicked her curls behind her ears. Freckles even on her earlobes.

The day she wore her hair up, Tibor yearned to put his solid, calloused hand on the back of her neck, letting it rest under the escaping tendrils as one might luxuriate behind a tropical waterfall. He could not suppress an odd desire: he wanted her to pay attention to him, not Chia. Foolish old man, he chided himself, stop thinking Nurit crossed your path thirty-five years too late. Yeah, but I could have set her straight. Yeah, nothing, he reminded himself, her affections are for the blue-haired one, who, to his mild surprise, was proving to be a hard worker, and unflinching.

It was Chia who placed "Stepped On" onto the workbench. He could no longer put it off. They lifted the lid to the cello case together, becoming equally nauseated at the mangled body before them. "Stupid kids," Tibor grumbled, steadying himself against the counter.

Tibor loosened the tailpiece and carefully unfastened the strings, moving the instrument gently, as one would a sick or dying child. He noticed the surreptitious way Chia wiped her eyes. She pressed her lips together and blinked rapidly. "Jesus…"

Tibor rubbed his forehead and sighed. "She still has vital signs."

He took a fine chisel and began working at the varnish along the seams between the instrument's top and sides. He dipped a cotton-tipped swab into alcohol and showed Chia how to run it lightly along the seams, how the alcohol would loosen the edges. He slid a spatula through the top and sides. Together they eased the broken top off the cello.

"Top's made of spruce," Tibor said. "Springy and strong. It's what the best instruments have for the top. Bridge, sides, neck, scroll…all maple. Fingerboard and tailpiece are ebony. Different elements make one extraordinary creation."

"Like people," Chia mused.

"Soundpost looks good," Tibor muttered, face inside the instrument. He was not going to get poetic with her.

He showed her how to lightly sand the sides of the cello before gluing on a new top. His twitchy hands felt cold and clammy from the intensity of the operation. When they finished, he sent Chia downstairs to the cafeteria to get him coffee. He waited by the sink, running warm water over his hands.

She returned with two cups. Curling his fingers around the warm paper, he felt better, jovial even. Surgery had gone well. Now he could be social.

"I was going to find you a nice Jewish boy, but it looks like you've gone and found a nice Jewish girl." Tibor wanted to make sure he was right. Fortuna had told him "partner" could mean any number of things these days.

Chia looked at him with a crooked grin. He waited for her usual flip response. "Judaism says God is infinite, so there must be infinite ways to approach God."

Sure sounded like she was lecturing him. "What's that supposed to mean?"

"Don't you think all that infinite-ness extends to God's works? Why not infinite ways to love God's creatures?"

A Yiddishe kop, Jewish smarts, thought Tibor.

Chia set down her coffee cup with the studied movement of a prosecutor. "Half the stuff in the Torah isn't relevant today. When was the last time you burned a red heifer to expiate your sins?"

"How do you know so much?" Tibor demanded. She had gone from impressive to insolent.

"I'm majoring in Feminist Jewish Instrument Repair Studies."

Chia did not appear to be making a joke. Tibor made his "aakkhh" sound and tossed his empty coffee cup away.

"Next," he called loudly, addressing the waiting shelves of instruments.

◇◇◇◇◇◇◇◇◇◇◇◇◇◇◇◇◇

By August, workers from the nearby offices were regularly bringing chairs over to listen to Nurit and Chia practice. The girls' repertoire and admiring listeners had expanded. The number of instrument repair projects had diminished. Instead of growing crankier as Labor Day approached, Tibor had the unheard-of luxury of reading articles in trade journals. He set up a lunchtime concert by the girls during Chia's last week. Fortuna and the grandsons and nearly everyone in the building came.

After the concert, Tibor planted a kiss on Nurit's sweaty, freckle-speckled hand, holding it perhaps a moment longer than was proper, in order to follow the sprinkles up to her armpit where they disappeared into a majesty of crinkly black hair. The school administrator who had placed Chia with him in June hurried over.

"It ended up working out so well," she gushed.

∞∞∞∞∞∞∞∞∞∞∞∞∞∞∞

Thursday afternoon before the holiday weekend, Tibor and Chia shook hands before parting.

"Where's Nurit?"

"Home packing. We leave for Rochester on Sunday."

Tibor folded his arms. All the paperwork had been filled out, all the instruments finished. Soon he would go home to work in the garden, go to *shul*, have a barbeque. He tamped down an uneasy stirring, a wistful ache to feel again what it meant to begin.

The following Tuesday morning Tibor had an extra cup of coffee at home and read the newspaper. From his garden he plucked ripe cherry tomatoes, some for his lunch, some for Fortuna still asleep upstairs. He got to work a good hour later than usual.

He took a moment to appreciate the Olympic Mountains to the west, blue-gray hulks still cradling a few scoops of snow. A growing list in his head crowded out the view: supplies to be ordered, band directors to be called, instrument placements finalized. Oh, yes, and the viola.

Tibor took down the case. Kind of light. He lifted the lid and stared dumbly. No viola, no bow, only a note pinned to the plush green lining. He recognized Chia's handwriting.

"Dear Tibor,

I have erred on the side of Eros. Please forgive me. When we are rich and famous, we'll pay you back.

Shalom, Conchita"

Dammit, a *ganef!* She'd taken the viola for her partner and run off. Run off with Seattle School District property. Tibor didn't know whom to call first, Security or Fortuna.

He lifted the phone to call home and set it down. Fortuna would orally corner him: "Who's to say the viola didn't come to you so you could give it to the girl? Why do young people have to wait until they're old and their passions tempered, before they can afford something beautiful? It's like those old guys driving their fancy sports cars—a young person should have such pleasure."

Tibor looked up the number for Security. He considered the police reports he would have to fill out and all the questions from the dolts in District Security. The custodians would get in trouble. The girls would be tracked down. They would say they had misunderstood and thought the summer-long viola loan was a long-term one. He would look like a fool for having trusted them. Locks would be changed. Who knew what else? And, there would be Fortuna's constant commentary.

Only he and the girls would know, if he said nothing.

A long morning ticked by before Tibor ate his lunch. A drowsy afternoon followed.

A few minutes before five, Tibor took down his master logbook. He turned to the viola section.

Concentrating on keeping his fingers from giving away his doubts, from acknowledging the flicker of vengeance as well as the illusory longings, he wrote next to an entry: *Beyond repair, salvaged for parts.*

He closed the logbook. The peachy beginnings of a sunset filled the workshop and washed over Tibor, his face alight with recognition. Little Eli's celestial description of the place had indeed been apt.

Take, tsvei ganeyvim in himmel, in truth, there had been two thieves in heaven, Tibor thought, walking past the empty practice rooms. One had stolen a viola. The other had helped herself to his heart.

About to descend the stairs, he stopped briefly to open and close a mental door to a dark, dusty closet — where his parents' grim stories resided, where the despair and indignities of being poor immigrants had been shoved, where his hurts hung. To that place did Tibor banish any further thoughts of the day's discovery.

Slubs

The fabric store's mirrors reflected a plump trio: a coffee-bean brown man, a walrus-mustachioed white man, and a young woman, her skin a perfect blend of the two. Except for the gender impossibility, she could have been their daughter.

Clay, the dark brown one, held up a bolt of turquoise taffeta, as hirsute Barry draped it around Eve's waist and legs.

Eve giggled into her hand. "I look like a fat Statue of Liberty."

"Not fat — *zaftig*," Barry corrected. Around his neck dangled a pair of scissors and a Star of David, equal in size.

Clay looked at the material and at his own reflection. "Turquoise works for my skin tone."

"And everything has to be about you?" Barry teased.

The fabric store owner figured "the seamsters," as she called these regular, gay customers, wouldn't mind her intervention. "Something darker would be more flattering. What's your budget?" The owner led them to the silk section and pulled out a bolt of dupioni, a navy-green mix, iridescent as a dragonfly. Eve did not want to appear too eager. *God bless the child that's got its own.* Clay and Barry exchanged looks above her — more than twice what they had thought to spend.

The trio returned with the store owner to the mirrors. All four nodded in agreement over the color and the fabric. "A *shiddach!*" A match! Barry clasped his hands together like a newly informed in-law. Eve allowed herself a full smile. "I love it."

Barry and the store owner fanned out for thread, a zipper, and lining.

"I feel like Cinderella," Eve chortled.

"Every girl needs a *fairy* godfather, chile." Clay pretended to tap her on the head with a wand. He wished Jolene, Eve's mother, could see the teenager's unabashed glee. Clay and Barry designed for drag queen shows, a surprisingly lucrative endeavor on the West Coast, where corporations and non-profits used such entertainment for holiday parties and fundraisers. The pair gave back by designing gratis for Seattle-area high school musicals. Clay also accepted requests to join high school audition committees, thrilled to help set in motion a new show and uncover a teen diamond in the rough like senior Eve Larson.

⬦⬦⬦⬦⬦⬦⬦⬦⬦⬦⬦⬦⬦⬦⬦

Clay had first seen Eve in a formless sweatshirt and ripped black skirt. She'd stood apart from the chummy clumps of other auditioning kids. Before disappearing behind the band room door, Clay had given her a go-get-'em grin, maybe because of her tawny skin color, maybe because of her size.

Clay got a better look when Eve stepped in front of the audition commit-tee. Thirty pounds lighter, she would have been statuesque; seventy pounds lighter, a runway model. She had the profile of a Roman noblewoman, the insecurities of a circus fat lady. He wondered how she squeezed in and out of high school desks. By his own senior year in high school, he'd no longer fit in a desk. He'd sat in a chair at a long table, his stomach pouring over his belt. Two chins, three butts. In Eve, Clay recognized his awkward teenaged self.

Eve had shifted from foot to foot. The musical director had asked her what she would sing—asked twice, so faint was the reply.

"*You can help yourself, but don't take too much.*" A voice filled with shame and longing filled the band room. She sang Billie Holiday's words with her eyes shut, unaware that her soul was on exhibit. When Eve closed her trem-bling mouth and looked around, the audition committee members exhaled audibly.

Thank you. We'll be in touch. Good job.

The band room door swung shut. The committee members erupted.

My God. Who is that? She's amazing. Where did she come from? We could build a show around that voice. We can't give her the romantic lead, she's too big. Would the Music Boosters sponsor her to Weight Watchers? She could lose some weight before the show opens.

"I found my self-esteem project for the year," Clay told Barry that night.

High school musicals were the best intervention Clay knew. Clay's high school counselor had finagled him into a musical's tech crew class, assuring Clay's graduation, and giving him a group of nonjudgmental peers.

Driving home after a rehearsal, Clay had listened to two girls anguish about dates.

"I've never been on one," he confided.

"Are you gay, Clay?" one girl had joked, providing an explanation that had for so long eluded him.

Unable to shake his conventional late-1950s upbringing, he'd waited years before setting foot in a gay bar. He learned to like himself and began exercising. He'd gotten lazy in his forties and now, pushing fifty, was heading back towards pudgy. With years of experience dressing and sewing for stars in professional musical theatre, Clay knew how to camouflage the most unsightly bodies, including his own.

Eve landed a secondary role in the musical. Clay created an outfit for her far more form-hugging than she would have worn on her own. "Ain't nobody who doesn't love a full pantry," he insisted, eventually coaxing her into the sateen gown and out of hiding behind other cast members. Eve belted out her one big number with growing confidence. That girl is really getting into it, Clay had rejoiced each night. By the last performance, the audience demanded Eve take an extra bow.

"You sang real pretty, Eve." At the closing night reception, Jolene Larson beamed with quiet pride for her daughter. Nobody on her family's side of Eastern Washington wheat farmers had gone beyond an aimless whistle. Jolene wished she was more comfortable around these gregarious theatre people and the exuberant parents with their big gestures and gushy voices.

A chunky black man came up to her. "You must be Eve's mother." Her small, white hand disappeared into his dark clasp. She noticed the man wore eye shadow and mascara. He introduced himself, Clay Hastings. Jolene didn't think he'd been on stage and couldn't think why he'd be wearing make-up. Maybe in solidarity with the performing kids? She traded some polite words before edging away to wait by the doors for her daughter.

A few weeks after the show closed, Clay and Barry had presented Eve with a list of college music scholarships and two skirts of muted colors, extracting a promise from her to toss the ratty black *shmatte* in which Clay had first seen her.

In late February, Clay had called Jolene about his next project — a senior prom dress for Eve. The musical gown and the skirts had been thrown together in the band room at school. A prom dress would require more precise work, best done in their studio. Would Jolene be willing to ferry Eve to fittings, he wondered, since Eve did not drive. (No money for a Driver's Ed course, Eve had let slip.)

"If we make her a dress, she'll have to go to the prom," Clay reasoned with Jolene. "I'd offer her one of mine, but we're not the same size."

Jolene wasn't sure she'd heard right. She moved to known territory: how much were they thinking of spending? She was a single mother after all.

Clay brushed aside her misgivings. "We'll work something out." He scheduled the fabric store trip with Eve while Jolene was at her newspaper circulation job. If she didn't know the cost of materials, he reckoned, neither of them had to courteously decline or insist on payment.

◇◇◇◇◇◇◇◇◇◇◇◇◇◇◇◇◇◇◇

College costs were Jolene's foremost financial worry. With a weary sigh, she dropped mail on the kitchen counter the evening of Eve's trip to the fabric shop with Clay and Barry. "Wish we'd hear back from the schools."

Eve played with the envelopes. "I've been meaning to tell you." She paused and looked away. "I got accepted to The New School for Jazz."

"New York?" Jolene's mouth pulled down.

"I'm excited. Can't you be happy too?"

"It's so far away, so expensive."

Eve threw up her arms. "As a matter of fact, they gave me a huge scholarship. I got the letter and there was nobody here to tell and none of my friends were answering their cell phones." Squall-like sobs rolled out of her.

Jolene thought to put an arm around Eve. Instead, in her farmer father's oft-repeated words, she decided it was one of those "If it don't kill ya, it'll make ya stronger" moments. Jolene wagged a finger. "Here's a piece of advice I learned way too late — internal validation. Don't wait for other people to validate you. "

"Yeah, I'd have to wait forever for you," Eve bellowed.

"No decisions until we hear back from the other schools."

Eve dropped her eyes. "I didn't send in any other applications. I didn't think we could afford it." Jolene's mouth moved oddly, like an unhooked fish dropped to a dinghy's floor. She rocked forward.

"And what if you hadn't gotten in?"

Eve dismissed the question with a silent rise of her shoulders.

◇◇◇◇◇◇◇◇◇◇◇◇◇◇◇◇◇◇◇

Jolene and Eve were in Clay and Barry's studio for a final prom dress fitting. Jolene's eyes flicked to a gallery of large, framed photos of heavily made-up, amply built women. One looked like Barry.

Pins between his lips, Clay nattered away. Jolene feared he might accidentally swallow one, might need her help in extracting it.

"I think fashion designers are basically lazy. What's with sizes two to four? The real challenge is designing for plus sizes — how do I make a big girl feel like a million bucks? What do I do for someone who's hippy? Or, who has a large bust or lots of curves?"

"And who's not in favor of more curves?" Barry leered, thread in his teeth.

Clay eased the basted dress, straps not yet secured, over Eve's head. Jolene felt a jangle of envy watching the men's hands, like corpulent butterflies seeking a place to alight on her daughter.

Eve brushed the ruched bodice. "I thought the top part was going to be longer." Jolene could tell that what Eve saw in the mirror was not to her liking, not like Clay's first breathtaking sketches the girl had taped to the bathroom mirror at home. Eve attempted a breezy tone. "And I don't know about these ruffles." She picked at the skirt's offending section.

Jolene cast a wary look at her daughter, recognizing a familiar struggle — be grateful or be honest. *A crust of bread and such.*

Clay pulled at a bubbly seam. "A little dupioni goes a long, long way. You'd look top-heavy if we used more. Did you know that dupioni means double silk? When cultivated silkworms spin their cocoons, they produce rough, uneven filament — slubs — because they live more crowded than the wild ones, and their cocoons get tangled."

Jolene noted the way Clay glossed over Eve's distress. Eve not-so-discreetly tugged at her waist when Clay turned away.

Barry pulled back. "We need her in heels if we're going to get an accurate hem measurement."

Clay reached for a pair of black pumps. "Try mine." Jolene felt her stomach fold in a funny way.

Clay pinned the dress straps. "There's one more thing." From a pouch, he pulled out rhinestone earrings and a sparkly necklace. "We were looking for something for ourselves. We saw these and knew they were meant to go with your dress." Clay's delight in dolling her up was that of an indulgent father. Eve momentarily forgot her displeasure.

Jolene sat down. These men were beyond the understanding of a farm girl like her. She found Clay and Barry kind but unsettling, their city ways disturbing. They stood too close to you when they talked or said things they couldn't possibly mean. Jolene liked plenty of room and precious few words.

⬦⬦⬦⬦⬦⬦⬦⬦⬦⬦⬦⬦⬦⬦⬦⬦⬦

Jolene grew up about ten miles south of an intersection known as Humphrey's, in Washington's sparsely populated Palouse. She was happiest not sticking out — just working hard and living quietly. To have acquired such a noticeable daughter, with such dramatic associates, was social quicksand. This was not Jolene's world of self-effacing young women who made do, who made themselves small. Where had it gone?

Jolene knew about pitching in, about summer wheat and winter wheat, about being careful with a dollar. She had toiled alongside her brothers, father, and the hired Hispanic workers on the farm.

At a gym teacher's urging, she'd tried out for her high school's cross-country team. She loved moving her sturdy body towards the far spaces, joined occasionally by a surprised coyote or a scurrying covey of quails. Her rhythmic breathing, the pump and pull of arms and legs put her above the undulating Palouse and somewhere between earth and sky, existence refined to essential electrical impulses.

Jolene accepted a coach's offer to run for a college in Spokane, two hours away from home. There she met Dewayne, a jive-talking sprinter, impressed with her long-distance running and her rear. "So tight you could serve lemonade on it," was his appreciative view of her behind from behind — his preferred position. The guy had bolted, was long gone, before Jolene'd realized that even with her irregular periods and low body fat, sperm and egg had persevered. She'd dropped out of college and come home to give birth, crying nearly as much as her bi-racial baby.

Jolene had wanted to name the girl Ila, after her pioneer great-grandmother. Her father's dry rebuke — "Don't seem like all that fittin' a tribute" — sent her off in uncharacteristic pique to the family Bible and its recorded generations of Larsons. She'd gone on to search for willful heroines in the text. Eve beat out Salome.

Her growing daughter was a daily reminder of an absence which cast a dark shadow over them both. Jolene had decided moving to Seattle, taking her conspicuous child away from small-town stares, would grant them the anonymity she craved. Her parents were not uncaring. Neither did they beg her to stay. They'd given Jolene money for first and last month's rent and people to contact.

"I'm just not sure how I feel about Eve," Jolene's mother had apologized.

With her first paycheck, Jolene had bought groceries, disposable diapers, and a used jogging stroller. After her shift answering phones for the city newspaper's circulation department, she'd suit up and strap Eve into the stroller with a cache of milk bottles, water, and snacks. They zipped down Capitol Hill and through Seattle's North End until houses gave way to truck farms and pasture. Jolene promised Eve they would see cows and horses. Eve sang joyful nonsense songs.

Locked in love and locomotion, they were horse and rider or magical queen and princess, parting eddies of moist Northwest air. Having run off every last sorrow, Jolene would turn the stroller around in the oyster light and jog languidly back to town. By the time they got home, Eve lay silent under a beloved blankie, the day gone dusky and cool.

Jolene would carry Eve into the bed they shared, blessing the exhaustion that allowed the child, a moist furnace, to stay curled in her arms all night. She'd place her face close to Eve's sweet, ephemeral breaths and watch the tiny pulse in the girl's neck. Morning's swift arrival always surprised Jolene, reluctant to release her daughter into the world.

Rain or shine, Jolene ran and Eve sang. Neighbors loaned them tapes of The Supremes, Aretha, Etta, Sarah, Billie, and Ella. "Bring your child up hearing her people," they'd said. Eve had no trouble embracing new mothers, black mothers, in the apartment complex.

The day finally came when Eve objected to being crammed in the stroller. An elderly neighbor, Auntie Coco, agreed to watch her during Jolene's long runs, but the runs got shorter and shorter. It wasn't the same for Jolene without Eve. It wasn't the same in general.

I want you to cook like Auntie Coco, Eve had demanded.

Jolene pushed back. Who puts honey on potatoes? Since when did you start loving rice pudding so much? Collard greens? Food became a battlefield.

Eve moved out of her mother's room and into the second bedroom. In time, that bedroom turned into a tumult of dirty dishes and empty chip bags. Jolene's purchase of a scale for the eleven-year-old set off a firestorm. And, as the girl headed into her teens, it seemed to Jolene that Eve was drawn to every glib black man who crossed her path.

◇◇◇◇◇◇◇◇◇◇◇◇◇◇◇◇◇

Eve's final twirl in front of the studio's full-length mirror elicited peeps of excitement from Barry. Clay, looking to Jolene for approval, saw her attention was elsewhere. He took in her unguarded scrutiny of the photos on the wall and pointed. "That one's me."

Jolene peered at a buxom black diva. She had to ask. "Does the school know you're gay?"

"Mo-ther." Eve looked at the ceiling.

"Let's just say I'm good at context shifting." Clay's voice was careful. "I've always endeavored to not be a stereotype; I like to show people I can be gay but not be flaming, so I'm different at work than at home than at school. You learn how to flip a switch. The kids see me dish one minute, yell like a drill sergeant the next."

"Nobody's said anything about you working with kids?" Surely, other parents must share her disquiet, Jolene supposed.

Eight eyes blinked, the only movement in the room until Barry's hand came up over his cheek, communicating mock shock. Clay cleared his throat. Jolene teetered on the edge of her chair. Eve teetered in Clay's shoes. Ever so slowly, as if extracting his phrases from a prickle bush, Clay spoke. "What you do to develop the next generation is really the only thing that lasts. Parents know this. They get to do it. I don't have kids, so I do it for the ones I can."

Jolene nodded politely, mortified. As trying as life with Eve could be, it would be far worse without her.

◇◇◇◇◇◇◇◇◇◇◇◇◇◇◇◇◇◇◇

The afternoon of the prom, Clay and Barry came over to the Larson apartment for photos, bringing with them a wrist corsage and a brand-new digital camera for Eve. Jolene's balcony roses provided a fragrant backdrop for the various poses — Jolene and Eve, Clay and Barry and Eve, Eve alone, hamming it up, and finally, a cautious Jolene between Clay and Barry.

Clay and Barry had paid a hair dresser friend to straighten Eve's hair into an elegant updo. The stylist had applied tasteful make-up, too, Jolene admitted, blinking rapidly behind the upheld camera. She didn't know what to do with the squirmy gratitude welling up inside and coming out her eyes. Eve's dramatic sighs also must be from the heightened emotions and excitement, Jolene figured.

Eve waved to a few gawkers on other balconies, reveling in their catcalls. Jolene had a playful vision of beautifully dressed girls waving from each balcony, eclipsing the detritus of rusted barbeques and cracked plastic chairs. What a sight: hundreds of rippling, gem-colored dresses, like proud banners, rallying the gray apartment dwellers to look past jaded lives and, wide-eyed, encounter wonder.

Eve kept adjusting the dress. Something felt awry to Jolene. "We'll be right back." Jolene reached for Eve's hand and led her into the bathroom. "What's wrong?"

"I can't wear this and I don't want them here when my friends come," Eve whispered.

Jolene's shoulders sagged. Fickle teenager. Double-crossing, cold-hearted, rotten teenager. "That's hardly fair," she whispered back, "considering all the work they went through for you. You should have said something sooner."

"I tried to, they wouldn't listen. They got their pictures. They can leave now."

"You're being ridiculous."

Eve stomped out of the bathroom and over to Barry and Clay who were smoking on the balcony. "My mother doesn't allow people to smoke here." Jolene opened her mouth and closed it again, thought unsaid. Eve would use anything to her advantage.

"We should be going anyway. Have a grand time, Gorgeous." Barry's necklaces clinked as he bent to kiss Eve. Jolene extended her hand to ward off anything so intimate. Barry took it with a small bow. Clay winked at Eve. "Look like a million bucks." His work was done.

With the door's closing click, Eve sped down the hall. "Quick, unzip me."

Jolene, surprised by this rare alacrity in her offspring, did what she was told. Eve stepped out of the dress. "I totally can't go to the prom in this. It's not me. It's them. I look like a parade float, like a freakin' Jolly Green Giant on a parade float. I didn't want to hurt their feelings, but it didn't turn out like how I thought it would."

Jolene was in a dither. She doubted she could prevail on Eve to carry on in the martyr tradition of the Larson women. She resorted to sarcasm à la Barry. "You were expecting some little black number?"

"It's so over the top."

Jolene snatched the dress from the hall floor. "I think that's the way gay men do things."

Eve disappeared into her room, emerging in a plain black top and one of the skirts Clay and Barry had made her in the fall. The rhinestones stayed in place. Jolene slumped against the wall, arms crossed. "They'll be so disappointed."

"They don't need to know," Eve said with an airy flick of her wrist, a Clay gesture Jolene recognized. No doubt there were things Eve had decided Jolene didn't need to know either. While leaving a pile of clean underwear on the girl's dresser, Jolene, frustrated by such little knowledge of her daughter, had taken a cursory peek in the top drawer. There she'd found an empty vodka bottle and a condom. Jolene hadn't yet figured out a way to mention the discovery without exposing herself.

The buzzer rang—Eve's friends. Two tuxedoed young men and a skimpily dressed girl Jolene recognized from the musical came into the apartment. Jolene stashed the prom dress on a hook behind the bathroom door. One of the boys hailed Eve. "You look great." Jolene bit the inside of her lip. *You should have seen her before.*

After a whirl of more photos, the young people pranced out to the elevator, followed by a servile Jolene. At the waiting limousine, other kids were standing up through the vehicle's sunroof.

Jolene had gotten out of Eve that the evening included a fancy restaurant before and a hotel suite after the dance. Jolene had strenuously objected to the hotel part of the evening, worried about cost as much as possible sex. This drew a snigger from Eve: Clay and Barry had slipped her money—a lot of money—to pay for these extravagances.

The white limo pulled away. Jolene hesitated before waving. No one waved back.

Jolene walked up the stairs and into the apartment, drawn to the prom dress. Relieved of its young wearer's intensity, the gown's glistening green soothed her, slaked a vague thirst. She unbuttoned her shirt and slid off her jeans. She hardly ever wore dresses. No reason to dress up, or to feel feminine. She worked her way into the garment. She scrunched a ball of material in back to tighten the waist and looked into the mirror. It wasn't so awful.

She stroked the dupioni's nubs. No, Clay had called them slubs. It amused her, knowing what slubs were — probably the first person from around Humphrey to have ever used the word knowledgeably. She thought about Clay, Barry, Eve, and herself over the past year, their encounters like slubs in a bumpy fabric of human coexistence. Jolene hung the dress in her closet. What she would have given for someone to have made such a fine fuss over her.

She flicked the television on and off, opened and closed the refrigerator, brushed a few crumbs off the dining room table. She sought the companionable silence of the roses on the balcony, a balcony different from the neighboring ones packed with bikes, drying racks, and baby strollers. Maybe she did have a streak of the other in her.

An odd desire propelled her back inside. She rode the elevator down to storage. It had been years since she had given any thought to the jogging stroller. She turned on the lights and saw the worn, spongy handles. It felt good to grip something firmly. She rummaged through the stroller's pouch, finding artifacts from a long-ago life — small mittens, dried-out wet wipes.

She brought the stroller outside and began walking, no destination in mind initially. She did a little skip. She wasn't wearing running shoes, wasn't dressed for a workout. The skip led to an easy jog. It had been years. "Like getting back on a horse," her father's voice said in her head. The swish of her hair flagging behind her was a sound nearly forgotten.

She kept jogging. "Going to pick up my daughter," she fibbed to a woman also waiting for the traffic light to change. The pretense made Jolene smile, a flicker of appreciation for Clay and Barry's affectations. She ran through the Arboretum. She ran across Montlake Bridge and headed north on the Burke-Gilman Trail. Street lights came on. She walked long enough to catch her breath and plodded on. She was shocked at all the development north of the city. The truck farm she was looking for was covered with skinny houses. No cows or horses anywhere. Deflated, no longer eager to look for the past, she changed direction, blistered feet returning her to the quiet apartment well past midnight.

Jolene rode up in the elevator with the stroller. She put it on one side of the apartment's small entryway before collapsing into bed. Her legs twitched involuntarily as sleep overtook her, her breath and heartbeat lulling and familiar, like rushing wind, like steady, rubber footfalls.

A Dangerous Dance

Every dance has a Mr. Smooth, an elderly gentleman who effortlessly steers novices around the floor with nary a skid mark.

He pursues the full body press of firm female flesh. He's well-appointed. His face is smooth and shiny. He's dressed in a pressed, short-sleeved cotton shirt and smells faintly of mint breath freshener and aftershave. He coos instructions: "Lean back a little. Lift your elbows."

He avoids eye contact with his partner except to ask for a dance and thank her for it afterwards, for his mind's camera appears focused on himself. He's a dance god in supple leather character shoes, who draws a woman into his fantasy and feels no need to explain to her how or why.

Francine notices all this because the Mr. Smooth on the dance floor tonight has a past to which, in part, she is privy. Unlike other Mr. Smooths who, to dance-community newbies like her, seem to materialize on the dance floor like the fabled Olympians who sprang fully formed from Zeus's head, she and this Mr. Smooth sat together in Swedish class thirty years ago. From behind a protective three-deep corridor of partnerless women, she watches him pluck blondes.

It's an older crowd at the High Liner, a Fisherman's Terminal lunch place by day, dance joint by night. Women with thinning, colored hair, past their prime and wearing far less than what Francine considers tasteful, drape themselves over graying men. On the other side of the windows, rows of fishing boats rise like dark icebergs. The Zydeco music flows over the steamy dancers like a tide bringing in bad smells and questionable debris.

The band's lead singer, a sprout of gray hair sticking straight out from under his lower lip, wears his shirt unbuttoned low enough to reveal a flaccid white chest. He exhorts the crowd, "Raise your arms if what you really want for Christmas is more sex." The band's washboard player and drummer pound out an introduction for the next tune, setting the musicians and dancers in synchronized motion with the accordionist's rhythmic pushing, in-out-in-out. Couples of all permutations bump past Francine.

Francine, the last of the cell phone-less of her generation, decides she will wait only a few more minutes at the High Liner for her friends, co-workers at the high school. She wants the satisfaction of blatting at them, "Some waltz instruction."

Her single friends, Janet and Barb, had worn her down. Come dancing, they insisted. Lessons the first hour, band comes in and plays until midnight. Men outnumber women two to one. Francine wishes she had stayed home with a bottle of red wine.

Mr. Smooth stops in front of her and smiles broadly. "Fredericka?" Francine starts. "Lars!" Their Swedish class names.

"What on earth are you doing here?"

"Truthfully, I'm not sure. I don't know how to do this."

"Hold on." To her great discomfort, he pulls her onto the dance floor, where women in skin-tight jeans sit astride their partner's thighs. Francine is wearing a prim white top and polka-dotted skirt. She tries to keep space between her abdomen and his. Every time she eases off, he pulls her back.

The tune ends. "Had as much fun as you can stand?" Lars, really Larry, wipes his forehead with a handkerchief. To Francine, it is the first genteel action in an undulating sea of foreplay.

"It's a little shocking," she croaks.

"Yeah, it's been called a substitute for sex."

How clinical, Francine thinks. "I'm supposed to meet friends here."

"Don't worry about it. I'll buy you a beer." Francine is not a big beer drinker, especially on cold nights in December. "Coffee, please."

In the lighted area away from the dance floor, Larry comes back with drinks and sits down across from her. Francine gets a better look. What's left of his hair is white and wispy.

"You were off to Sweden the last time I saw you," she says. Larry is in the middle of a huge swallow, giving her a moment to recall her curiosity about the only other dark-eyed, dark-haired student among the fair-skinned Swedish majors.

She had enjoyed his surprise when, on the first day of class, she'd told him Swedish was her first language. For her the class was going to be an easy A. "One of my grandmothers was a Swede. She got my mother and my aunts, as little girls, out of Berlin and up to Sweden. My grandfather was a Russian Jew, and the Nazis forced them to divorce. The Swedes were good to my people. Why are you here?"

Larry had smiled slyly, "Swedish women."

Awfully full of himself, Francine had decided.

At the table with her now, Larry wipes beer foam from his mouth. "There was a particular Swedish woman. However, when I got to Stockholm, turns out she was taken. I sat around in the coffee shops on Karlavägen for a few weeks and let some long-legged natives heal my heart before heading home to a brighter future."

Francine regards him. Still full of himself.

"And what should I know about you?" Larry asks.

"I work in a high school attendance office and have two daughters in college."

"Is there a man in your life?"

"My husband's in a nursing home, with Parkinson's." She knows it will be a conversation stopper.

"That's too bad." Larry eyes the dance floor. Francine isn't bothered by his retreat. She is used to people jumping back and out of a conversation once informed of her husband's state. Larry and Francine exchange e-mail addresses and a damp handshake.

"*Vi ses och hörs,*" Francine recalls. See you, we'll hear from you.

◇◇◇◇◇◇◇◇◇◇◇◇◇◇◇◇◇◇

"Francine, you dingbat, The High *Lighter*," sighs Janet the next day on the phone. "We wondered why you didn't show."

Francine leans back into her couch and ponders the possible meaning of this mix-up.

"Maybe I was supposed to meet someone."

Janet's voice goes up and down. "Ooh, who?"

"He's sixty-five." Francine feels as if she is chatting with a high school confidante, no doubt from being around teenagers and their constant dramas all week. "Do sixty-five-year-old men expect sex after a few dates?"

Janet titters. "Depends on how much Viagra they take."

Francine has not had sex for years. She misses it and she's caught herself staring at some of the good-looking senior boys. It's not like she could, or would, flirt with them, or even with the unmarried male teachers, all years younger than her. She grows faint-hearted thinking of sexual misadventures that might await even with a sixty-five-year-old. She is not eager to reveal her dimpled belly, her sagging breasts.

Janet says she will get more details back in the office on Monday. This distresses Francine. Honestly, she just met — re-met — the guy. Francine goes back to her computer and reads again the e-mail from Larry.

"You'll find waltzing more respectable than Zydeco. And the waltz beat is one almost everyone can relate to, because as a fetus we hear and are imprinted by our mother's heart rhythm. Truth? Dancehall legend?

"Keep in mind, when the waltz first appeared in late 1700s Europe, people were scandalized because the couple (gasp!) embraced. Parents were warned against exposing their daughters to 'so fatal a contagion.' In 1760, churches banned the waltz in Germany.

"I promise no harm will befall you by joining me in this 'dangerous' activity. Ha, ha. Larry."

Every day after Swedish class, Larry and Francine had chatted. She'd waited for an invitation to coffee or a walk through campus. Finally, Larry had asked her whether she needed housing over the summer. Confused, Francine thought for an instant he was asking her to move in with him. She learned he owned his own home and rented out several other houses. She had never met a landlord, much less had one for a classmate. To her, at age twenty-one, the possibility of dating an older landlord suddenly seemed abnormal, predatory on his part. Larry appeared mostly interested in her future financial worth to him, anyway. She decided she would interact with Larry in and around class, no further.

◇◇◇◇◇◇◇◇◇◇◇◇◇◇◇◇◇◇◇◇◇◇

The smells of plastic and uric acid assail Francine's nose when she drops by the care center after work. She has a CD player and a CD of medieval choral music for Danny. Danny doesn't allow her to leave anything in his room for fear — real or perceived — that it will be stolen. What she heard of the CD at work was simple and soothing, no discernible beat.

Danny waits in his wheelchair. She kisses his cheek and hugs his bony shoulders. The man is wasting away. He has lost more than fifty pounds from a hideously early onset of Parkinson's. Two years ago, they made the wrenching decision to put him into the care home full time. She is relieved to see how calmly he sits, having timed her visit to coincide with his sedative.

Francine leaves her hand on his thin forearm. "These songs used to go on for days," she reads from the CD liner notes. "Time meant a very different thing to people in the Middle Ages. They didn't have clocks in every room." Danny unsteadily raises his bare right wrist, a silent reminder that he relinquished his watch upon entering the care center. They listen to most of the CD before Francine attempts a light tone. "I tried going to a dance Saturday night."

Danny's head sways forward and back in an effort to mouth a response. "Wha-aat kind of mmmuu-sic?"

"The craziest thing — Zydeco. Really raucous. Actually, really raunchy. This CD is much nicer." Danny inclines his head toward the sweet angel voices. "Yes, I li-iike it."

Francine moves on, describing the neighborhood Christmas decorations, the surprising sprinkling of *hanukkiot* in some windows, college news from the girls, who will be home soon.

She plugs in an electric *hannukiah* and twists the little bulbs, cringing slightly at the garish orange glow. Tacky as all get out, but the care center does not allow candles. She will unplug it and bring it home at the end of her visit since Danny worries that it, too, might be stolen.

A hand drum is added to the next song. The following melody includes chimes and wood blocks. Francine hadn't listened this far. Danny twitches. "I don't thhhh-ink I should liii-sten to thhhh-is anymore." His big hands start kneading the armrests of the wheelchair. His knees jerk.

Francine looks at her watch. She's been visiting a long time. The medication is wearing off. She puts her hands on his shoulders as the dyskinesia, the involuntary movements, grow more violent. Fearing he will rock himself out of the chair, she checks his seatbelt. "It's faa-stened," Danny quavers. He becomes a whorl of arms and legs. She cannot keep talking in the face of this tumult, cannot keep her own chest from heaving. She turns off the CD player. "Danny, I'm going to step outside for a minute."

She grips the railing outside Danny's room and, hidden from his sight, leans her upper body towards the wall until her forehead feels a smooth coolness. After a time, composed, she bends her knees into a *plié*, back held straight. Then up on her toes, *relevé*. Up and down. Knees flex, knees lock. Feet flat, feet arch.

"Everything okay, Miss?" It is Amina, the new nurse's aide.

"I'm giving Danny and me a break. He gets so agitated," Francine whispers.

Amina nods. "Overstimulation. It's time for dinner and meds, anyway. You just keep dancing there, Miss." Francine thinks it is cute the way Amina, maybe in her mid-twenties, calls her Miss. Amina, smiling, does a shuffle, a quick-step and a shoulder roll before moving into Danny's room. Some African dance step, Francine presumes.

Francine likes the way Amina always takes Danny's hand when she enters the room. This past week Amina has been full of questions about the *hanukkiah*, eager to discuss the connections between her native Jamaica's Rastafarian culture and that of the Jews. "We're both descended from King David, eh?"

◇◇◇◇◇◇◇◇◇◇◇◇◇◇◇◇◇◇◇◇

Francine has evenings when she can't make up her mind who she should feel sorry for the most: Danny for his diminishing world, their daughters for the absence of a functioning father, or herself for the mid-life loss of male companionship. On the couch, she sips wine and slides her bare feet back and forth over the smooth wooden floor. She waits to be transported…to New Jersey.

She is pounding up the stairs to the East Orange dance studio with other girls in black leotards, all stick legs and arms at that age, like waves of scurrying beetles. The upstairs dressing rooms have small wooden benches and hooks, no lockers — in those days no one would think of stealing anything from anyone. The girls pull their hair back into tight ponytails. Chalk dust is stirred up every time someone enters or leaves. It hangs in the air, fine and milky. When the dressing room empties, Francine, not yet in toe shoes, furtively sticks the tip of her pink ballet slipper into a tray on the floor and raises it. The white chalk on the end looks like a milk moustache.

In the studio, a mound of a woman takes a last, long draw on a cigarette before running her fingers up the keyboard. The flourish of notes signals the girls to snuggle their feet into first position. Each girl grips the *barre* and arches back. Arms go up, to the side, and float down. The music of Chopin washes over them and lulls Francine to sleep.

◇◇◇◇◇◇◇◇◇◇◇◇◇◇◇◇◇◇◇◇

Larry compliments Francine on her poised frame — her raised arms and lowered shoulders are perfectly aligned. How light she is on her feet. He holds her gaze for a moment. "You're a natural dancer."

"My early ballet training." He desires me, Francine jokes to herself.

The band is packing up. Larry is doing something odd as he talks with Francine over his beer. Again and again, he pushes the folds back from his mouth up to his ears, pulling the skin taut, as if to show what his face once looked like.

Francine cannot keep her eyes open. She never stays up this late.

"You'd think with all the women I've escorted around a dance floor, I would have found one to marry. I've had lots of women friends, but no long-term intimate relationships."

There is something off about Larry, as if he is his own narrator. He tells Francine he used to dance six nights a week and compete. Now he works out at a gym to achieve that all-important maximum aerobic heart rate, lifts weights six days a week, dances twice a week. He doesn't need to wake up before noon.

"I guess I'm retired. I have boxes everywhere from the sale of my houses. Stuff that I just can't throw away or give away. I fixed everything myself, even looked after my renters — old Merchant Marines and alcoholics.

"I'd drive them to their doctor appointments and help them deposit disability payments. Closed a few estates. It was a good time, a time in my life when I felt the most needed."

Francine starts to put her hand on his arm as she once would have to console Danny. She catches herself and veers her hand to her mouth to cover a semi-real yawn. She shakes her head slightly. "I've spent the past five years caring for a sick husband and launching two daughters. I'm done being needed." Larry is being thick-headed about noticing her fatigue. He clunks down the empty beer stein.

"I really need to go," she declares.

Surprised, Larry jumps up. "Of course, let's get you home."

The ride in his pickup truck is silent. Francine is too tired to give much thought to appropriate leave-taking behavior. Larry walks her to the front door and steps with her into the house's entryway. Francine sticks out her hand. Larry does not shake because he is looking over her shoulder. "What happened to your furniture?"

The living room is empty, save for a couch. Shiny wooden floors extend from the entryway to the living room and wrap around into the dining room.

"It's easier to keep clean." Francine knows this sounds lame, but she's hesitant to say more. The floor is like a mirror, like a flat, wet surface for them to skim over. Francine is pleased she mopped it earlier.

"Really?" Larry doesn't believe her. "It would make a great space for dancing."

"I do practice some of my old ballet routines."

Larry pockets his keys and pulls her into the living room. "When I taught dancing, I'd always tell the leads, 'Bring your follow, usually the woman, in to you close with your left arm, and push her away with your right hand. Does that seem familiar, guys?'"

Francine snickers. It feels better to be tired in her living room than in the noisy bar. Larry walks her through several waltz turns, positioning her next to him, hip-to-hip. He teaches her a zig-zag move, finishing with a step in which he twirls her in front of him and she lands on his other side, again, hip-to-hip. She keeps her eyes on his shoulders and waits for him to stop and ease into a kiss.

"One more move." Larry counts 1,2,3,4,5,6. Francine feels a strange, soothing fluidity course through her. She closes her eyes. It is someone else guiding her now. His warm breath and perspiration-soaked shirt are a balm. She lays her head against his neck. Different smell. Her eyes struggle open to see with whom she is dancing. Startled, she pulls away from Larry and heads for the wine bottle on her kitchen counter. "May I pour you some?"

"A drop, and I'll mix it with some juice if you have it."

Francine grimaces: what a gauche thing to do to good wine. Larry lectures her on the longevity-enhancing aspects of drinking two ounces of red wine daily. "I don't particularly like the taste of wine," he laments. "When you get to be my age, all this stuff becomes important. Like, you're not supposed to do just crossword puzzles to keep your mind agile. You're supposed to do new and different things."

Francine lifts her glass. "*L'chaim.*"

Larry is not deterred. "Studies show that if men have sex at least three times a week, they live longer. Now for women, it's not the rate at which they have sex. It's how they rate it."

Francine snorts. "So if I only have sex once a month but it's divine, I'll live as long as you?"

"That's what the scientists say."

"You really have sex three times a week?" Wine after an evening of dancing works faster than usual, Francine notes.

" 'A man's reach should exceed his grasp' — Browning." Larry chugs his remaining wine/juice. "Last night, a woman I asked to dance started getting affectionate. Then she stopped and asked, 'How old are you anyway?' When I said sixty-five, she said, 'Too old for me.' Needless to say, I did not make my weekly goal."

"Yikes, that must have hurt." Francine keeps her gaze down, afraid she will laugh.

"No, I wasn't really hurt." Larry considers. "More like disappointed."

Francine snorts again. A machine, an automaton, as full of himself as ever. "*Oy vey,*" she sighs.

"That's Yiddish, isn't it? It's what my parents spoke when they didn't want me to understand what they were saying."

Francine narrows her eyes. Not in a million years. "You're Jewish?"

"My parents were."

"Your mother was Jewish?"

"She said she was."

"What kind of family was this?"

"My father died when I was seven and my mother checked out. I was perfectly happy raising myself. I haven't talked to my older brother in decades."

"No aunts or uncles or grandparents?"

"Not that I know of."

Francine sets her glass down. Too weird, too weird. In a stagy gesture toward the wall clock, she says, "It's so late. Let's continue this another time."

Larry exits the front door with neither a hug nor a handshake, and definitely no kiss.

Francine pours the remainder of the red wine into her glass and lowers herself onto the couch. She senses the darkened stage, feels the excitement of the young dancers as they adjust their tutus and tiaras. Her group is on next.

Suddenly, something is yanking her bun. Her partner has twirled in place too close to Francine. Her tiara has become stuck in Francine's hair.

Miss Markova's eagle eyes land on them. "Your hair is falling down," the instructor screams in a hoarse whisper.

The pianist hits an opening chord and the lights come up. Girls mince out on stage except for Francine and her partner, who are still attached. Miss Markova tears the tiaras off their heads and savagely re-pins their hair and their crowns before shoving them in the direction of the stage. Not only does she enter late, Francine, unnerved, trips over her own feet. Down she goes, down goes her partner. There is a gasp from the audience. Eyes burning, Francine runs back into the wings. Miss Markova, frozen smile on her face, grabs Francine's hand and dances her back out to the waiting partner. The two girls complete the piece with the rest of the class.

The next year, the steps Francine worked so hard to memorize fly out of her head. At the third recital, Miss Markova puts her in the back line. There is no fourth recital.

◇◇◇◇◇◇◇◇◇◇◇◇◇◇◇◇◇◇

Larry asks Francine to be his partner in a Seniors waltz competition. She feels a long-buried stir of fear. "I don't know," she dithers.

"Invite a dangerous person to tea."

"What?"

"Invite a dangerous concept into your life. It's one of the lines on a poster in my therapist's office. Do something outside your comfort zone."

He sees a therapist. Francine is unsure how this revelation affects her. She takes a week to give him her consent. They begin rehearsing in the high school gym after basketball practices; Francine can lock up with her school keys.

Larry counts into her ear. He stops her for the slightest infraction and makes her repeat a move correctly. In a few weeks, they are gliding about the gym seamlessly, their faces perfecting nonstop smiles. Judges prefer happy dancers, Larry tells her. Soon, Larry stops cueing Francine.

The week before the competition, they rehearse in their formal wear. Francine is bowled over by Larry in a tux and white gloves. He calls her a beautiful rose in her coral taffeta. The basketball players stay to watch, cheering at the end of the routine. "Way to go, Mrs. Sinsheimer! You rock!"

◇◇◇◇◇◇◇◇◇◇◇◇◇◇◇◇◇◇◇◇

Before stepping out of Larry's truck, Francine applies lipstick again, her heart revving up unnaturally. Her offer could prove to be a terrible mistake, even though Danny said he was eager to see. Well, the nurses had all hailed her idea of a demonstration before Larry and she head to the waltz competition. It seemed like a good idea to try it out.

Francine times the performance with Danny's medication cycle. He should be at his best. She hopes she will be.

"What if he starts crying or flailing? Or I do?" she moans. Larry faces her and, as if scripted, woodenly places his hands on her shoulders.

"We committed to doing this. Everyone will love seeing you in your gown."

"You're so unemotional. You assume we're going to be perfect."

Larry shrugs. "When I competed, people would ask me how I controlled my nerves. I would always say, 'Standing behind me is my teacher, and behind him is his teacher...' There was a sense of responsibility."

"You're standing behind me?"

"Yes and no. Actually, I will mostly stand in front of you," he responds earnestly. Francine gives him a playful swat. He looks at her, perplexed. "Did I say something wrong?"

"No, no. Here I am trying to get *you* to lighten up." She reaches for him and they sail down the hall, arm-in-arm, practicing their dance-competition smiles on the staff and residents.

Francine knocks on Danny's door. Clipped to his white shirt is a bow tie. From Amina, she learns. Francine blows out a sob and reaches for the wheelchair's handles, pushing Danny slowly down the hall to the dining area. Chairs and tables have been piled into a corner to create a dance floor on the bilious, paisley carpet. Nurses and aides position wheelchairs and their occupants around the area.

Francine waits for the final resident to be parked before turning on the CD player and walking with Larry to the center of the dining area. Waltz music barrels into the room. Larry holds her, strong and sure. They turn and her dress furls out. Larry's pomaded white hair disappears as he spins her away from him, comes back into view as he reels her in. She gives him a tentative smile. To Francine, the wheelchairs and their dull occupants whirl too. Nurses grab each other around solid midriffs and sway.

Slices of the room come together in Francine's vision like a giant kaleidoscope and flit away in a crescendo of sound and color. The music explodes and she soars. The final measures of music taper off, with Francine wrapped in Larry's arms, a womblike security. Then she sees Danny's eyes are closed. He *will* not see, she thinks, breathing hard.

The staff claps wildly. Francine kneels in front of Danny, his head wobbling as he draws himself up, his eyes reopened. "Don't brr—ing him ba—ack here."

Francine's sweaty smile contracts. She feels an old ache, a familiar unfairness. She wants to protest: I got it right this time, not one misstep, not one mishap. Even her elaborate updo has remained intact, hasn't caught on anything.

Amina comes over. "So beautiful! Isn't your wife great?" she croons.

Danny does not answer.

Francine looks for comfort from Amina, who fusses overlong with the wheelchair's brakes. Francine understands. Amina doesn't want to mix in — she will be here with Danny after Francine leaves.

"Danny, I'm not in love with him or anything. I'm not sleeping with him," Francine whispers, desperate. "I thought you would enjoy it."

Amina grips the wheelchair's handles. "We'll head back now. Best of luck, Miss!"

To the back of Danny's receding head, Francine, humiliated, wants to call: forgive me for being the healthy one, forgive me for dancing without you. Her pleas go unexpressed.

Larry holds out her coat. "You still want to compete, right?"

Francine needs to be angry at someone. "Thanks for asking," she spits out icily, spearing her hands into the coat sleeves. "I've just had the wind knocked out of me. You could be a little more understanding."

They walk without speaking to Larry's truck. Instead of turning the ignition key, Larry clenches the steering wheel. She can see his lips are pressed together.

"What?" She needs to have him take her home to her nonjudgmental bottle of red wine.

Larry looks over the steering wheel. "About five years ago, I went to a therapist over my not being able to relate well to people. What came out of it was his guess that I've been an undiagnosed case of Asperger's Syndrome all these years."

Francine is in no mood for some maudlin sick-off. Who's worse off? — Larry or Danny. "Isn't that a form of autism?"

"It's in the autism disorder spectrum. I try to follow the social cues and usually miss or mistake what other people get. I'm best at just acquiring a skill and perfecting it." Larry continues looking over the steering wheel.

Francine's shoulders rise loftily and fall with an accompanying, audible sigh. She places a hand over one of his hands on the steering wheel and brushes the other with a soft kiss. Larry starts up the truck, a wary smile growing. Francine wonders at the things she knows how to do without knowing.

◇◇◇◇◇◇◇◇◇◇◇◇◇◇◇◇◇◇◇

The morning after the dance competition, Francine puts on water for coffee; she has a strange desire to whisper to the plants and paintings and refrigerator pictures: "There's a man in the house. There's a man in the house." On the kitchen table lie the white gloves Larry wore the night before and the medals they received.

She listens for his awakening, startling at a strange sound. How long it has been since the toilet seat was lifted.

After shuffling around in the living room, Larry comes into the kitchen. "Good morning, Sunshine." So corny. She loves it.

"I've got a project for us," Larry informs Francine. She calls the care center to tell Amina to take over Danny's Sunday morning hygiene routine.

Larry and Francine pull into the Home Depot parking lot. Larry picks a measuring tape out of his tool box in the truck's back seat and leads Francine to the lumber department. He measures the long poles.

"Put your hand around it," he orders. "You like this diameter?" The chasm in Francine's throat keeps her from answering. She nods, bright-eyed.

Larry picks up brackets and screws and attaches a small red flag to the end of the pole, which sticks out the back of his pickup. "I'll varnish it first and then install it."

The following Sunday morning, Larry attaches the railing against the windowless wall of Francine's living room. She calls the care center to ask that Amina handle the hygiene routine again. Francine hangs up the phone and places her hand on the new *barre*. She stretches in each direction.

Larry's arms are folded across his midriff and his legs are apart (in second position, Francine observes). He watches her fingers curl around his handiwork. His solid upper body build and snug white T-shirt give him a pleased Mr. Smooth genie look.

Francine extends her hand to Larry and leans her head back slightly, humming an off-key approximation of a waltz, sure that no prima ballerina could take more pleasure than she from a partner's artistry. "*Tack så mycket.*" Thanks so much.

◇◇◇◇◇◇◇◇◇◇◇◇◇◇◇◇◇◇◇

A few miles north at the care center, Amina washes Danny's hair and shaves his face. He barely responds to her chatter. A male aide will clean him from the neck down.

After toweling and combing Danny's hair, Amina sits across from him to clip his nails. What a contrast these milky asparagus stalks are, she thinks, comparing them with the chubby, chocolate fingers her young son will soon clasp around her neck when she swoops him up after work. She will cradle her little boy's hands, as she now does Danny's, and kiss and name each finger, the way her mother did with her when she was little. "City slicker, pot licker, tall man, wedding dancer, and pinkie, winkie prancer."

Amina glances about before bringing Danny's thumb to her pursed lips. She gives a tiny kiss to his forefinger, middle finger, ring finger, pinkie. She sings the silly names softly.

She sets Danny's right hand down. He is staring at her. She has been warned in the past about attending too closely to a patient's needs. Has she overstepped her role?

It seems yes, until his hands — once able to race over piano keys, to hold growing daughters, to light candles each Hanukah, to whirl a loving wife across a dance floor — offer her a glimpse of a life-sustaining desire that resides even in the powerless.

Danny accepts her invitation. Silently, he lifts a trembling left hand toward her mouth.

Family Custom Tailor

A stubby, brown-eyed man jumped up from behind his sewing machine and waved his pointer finger at the swirl of scarf and long robe coming through the shop's front door. "Adel wife, Adel wife!"

He fired off some Arabic to a matronly, draped woman and gestured impatiently towards the waiting Sandra. He sat back down with a theatrical shake of his head.

"Can I help you?" The older woman's face was barely visible behind a snug *hijab*, her headscarf. The heavily accented English conjured up for Sandra, a mostly uncovered Everett homemaker, the dusty sun-baked stones of past trips to Israel.

The woman swished behind the counter and placed a measuring tape around her neck.

The walls of Family Custom Tailor were covered with calendars in Arabic, a yellowed Washington State business license, pictures of five beaming children, and newspaper articles featuring a distinguished-looking man with wavy black hair declaring his love for America and Palestine. The shadowy shop was stacked with bolts of cloth and racks of unfinished clothes. A flickering shoebox-sized black-and-white television sat on the counter.

Sandra's gaze settled on a faded photo of a smiling young woman, hair curly and coiffed, in a short skirt and sleeveless white blouse, a measuring tape around her neck.

"I've had this silk from Tashkent and I've always thought I'd do something with it, but it's been 10 years already. Doesn't look like that's going to happen. I was wondering if you could make me a jacket?"

"Put here." The woman tapped a wide work table behind the front counter. As Sandra unfolded the material, the woman moved her hands reverently across the rolls of gold.

"Beautiful, beautiful. How you want?"

Sandra pulled out a short, dressy jacket from her bag.

"I don't have a pattern. Something like this?"

The seamstress fingered the seams, lining, pockets and hem.

"I talk with my husband, but I think yes. Please, you leave this here."

"Do you need a deposit?" Sandra asked.

"No, not yet. My husband, he call you." The older woman smiled and held out a business card with a dark green drawing of a thimble, a scissors, needle and thread, and the name Adel Al Tirhi. Underneath the name was printed "Nothing is Impossible."

Several weeks later came a phone message from a honeyed, older man's voice.

"This is Adel Al Tirhi. Please, won't you come in for a fitting now. Any time, just come."

Sandra drove over to the shop. A gray-haired man with the bearing of a diplomat greeted her. Mr. Al Tirhi, the man in the clippings, brought out her material, now in pieces, and asked her to step to the back of the store by the mirrors so he could pin the jacket together.

The little man who had huffed at Mrs. Al Tirhi during Sandra's first visit opened the back door. He flicked away a cigarette butt and blew a blue cloud over his shoulder before coming in. He wedged himself behind a sewing machine and ignored the two of them.

Mr. Al Tirhi studied Sandra in the mirror. He pinned and tugged. He repinned and refolded, soothing murmurs following each adjustment.

"Your husband will find you most attractive in this," he whispered, his dark eyes daring. Sandra inclined her head, a queen acknowledging a court favorite's flattering predictions. Mr. Al Tirhi eased her out of the pinned-together jacket and guided her to the front counter, his hand cupped under her right elbow.

Sandra's stomach became a slow-motion fifty-foot wave. She could not meet Mr. Al Tirhi's silky gaze for the breaker crashing onto shore inside of her. She searched the counter for a diversion and played with a business card. He gently pulled it out of her hands and turned the card over. He readied his pen.

"What is your husband's name?"

Sandra wanted to say something exotic, wanted to captivate this man with his aging movie star looks. If only American husbands knew from such charm.

"Ken," she admitted, and watched him make a few squiggles...ah, Arabic...apparently "Ken and Sandra." Mr. Al Tirhi drew a heart around the two names.

"These two, in love forever."

Sandra felt the receding wave undermine sand from beneath her feet as it washed back out to sea. She gripped the counter's edge and stared at the photos on the wall to regain her composure.

"These are all your children?" she asked with a socialite smile, eyes wide.

"My four sons and one daughter. I think one day I will go back to Palestine, but my children are all grown and here and they are my life now." He raised an eyebrow and his shoulders, resigned but not unhappy.

"Congratulations on such a lovely family. I have three kids. They all go back to school next week. How do you say congratulations in Arabic?"

"*Mabruk!*"

"*Mabruk,*" Sandra echoed. "My people say *Mazel tov.*"

"I know. Good day."

Sandra had to come back in to the shop for her car keys. She was that distracted.

⬦⬦⬦⬦⬦⬦⬦⬦⬦⬦⬦⬦⬦⬦⬦

A fall full of school field trips, weekend birthday parties, and soccer games went by before Sandra realized she had not heard from Mr. Al Tirhi. She dialed the shop.

"Hallo?" It was the jarring voice of the little man.

"Mr. Al Tirhi, please."

"Not here."

"Is his wife in?"

"Not here. Both at hospital. They call you back." He hung up without getting her name or phone number.

Sandra tried again a few days later and got Mr. Al Tirhi's wife.

"My husband very sick," she said. "He work more slow. When can you come in?"

When Sandra showed up, Mr. Al Tirhi greeted her with a forced smile. He raised himself gingerly. He sat back down.

"I am only a little dizzy," he faltered. Supporting himself with one hand on the work table, he reached for the partially sewn jacket.

Sandra had neither seen skin so gray nor eyes so dull. She wanted to flee but stood stone-like and unnerved while he fit the jacket on her and stopped for shallow breaths. There was no conversation this time.

"I have it ready for you very soon," Mr. Al Tirhi assured her.

He's dying, Sandra guessed. I'll never see this jacket finished.

Weeks passed with no word from the tailor.

One morning on her way to a Hadassah book group, Sandra stopped by Family Custom Tailor. The cool Pacific Northwest mist did nothing to extinguish her slow burn. It was rude and unprofessional on their part not even to call, she fumed.

She got out of the car ready to scold. The front door of the dark shop was locked, a notice taped to the glass. "Owner in hospital. Sorry for any inconvenience." A phone number was listed. She knocked anyway.

Like a giant, curling fish, Mrs. Al Tirhi materialized from the depths of the store. She stood behind the notice and scrutinized Sandra before unlocking the door.

"I so glad to see you," she said, motioning Sandra towards the basted jacket hanging next to the mirrors.

Mrs. Al Tirhi helped Sandra into the garment. The shop was still. No television, no thick little man, no tinkling of bells on the front door. Just the two of them in wary silence.

Sandra's irritation withered. "How is your husband?" she ventured.

"He is home from the hospital. Cancer, stomach cancer." A long pause. "I tell him 'Adel, Adel, you must finish this jacket'…" Mrs. Al Tirhi broke off with a sob and Sandra felt her own eyes sting. Her dismay mounted as the older woman collapsed into a chair and wept without restraint.

In seconds that spanned centuries of uncertainty, Sandra put an arm around the distraught wife's shoulder. Mrs. Al Tirhi wiped her eyes and struggled out of the chair to finish the fitting, seemingly revived, if not a little embarrassed. "*In shaa' al-laah, in shaa' al-laah*, God willing, God willing," she murmured over and over.

When Sandra left, she jotted down the phone number on the notice outside the store.

Marine fog gave way to cold rain and then to the frost of November. Sandra dug through her wallet for a phone number. A young man answered, Ahmed, the second of Mr. Al Tirhi's sons, she learned.

"My father died five days ago."

Ahmed said he was aware of Sandra's unfinished jacket and apologized for the delay, his voice smoother yet than his father's, she thought. He and his brothers were trying to return the remaining clothes. The business was up for sale and the shop closed. Certainly his mother could not run it.

"My father was one of the first Arab merchants in Everett," Ahmed told her. "He shooed his children away from the needle and thread and into college. When my mother is able, she will bring you the jacket," he promised.

"There's no rush," Sandra lied politely. "My little jacket's not a big thing compared with what you're going through." She had hoped to wear it to a splashy synagogue fundraiser that weekend, four months after she had first walked into Mr. Al Tirhi's shop.

When Mr. Al Tirhi's daughter, Halima, called, Sandra was struck by her diction, a feminine version of the undulating speech of the Al Tirhi men. "Hello, Mrs. Sandra? Your jacket is finished. My mother and I would like to come by your house this evening."

Their knock on the door brought Sandra's two daughters, son, and the terrier bounding into the large, tiled entryway. Mrs. Al Tirhi and a stylish young woman in jeans waited outside, arm-in-arm. The children stared through the window at the older woman's white and brown hijab and floor-length robes.

"Is she a wizard?" asked the boy, a seven-year-old Harry Potter fan.

Sandra opened the door. Mrs. Al Tirhi nodded and lowered her gaze. The young woman gave Sandra a friendly smile. "I am Halima." A stunning girl, with her father's amatory eyes.

"I'm sorry for your loss," Sandra started to say. "It's so kind of you to come to my home." She stopped, suddenly confused. Was this a business or social call? Maybe she should offer tea. Would they drink in her house?

"*In shaa' al-laah, in shaa' al-laah,*" the older woman began intoning. She made no move to hand over the shimmering jacket under the plastic wrap, turning instead to Halima and speaking quietly in Arabic. Sandra's son backed away, fearful of this stranger in his house. "Is she making a spell?" he whispered.

"My mother is reluctant to give you this colorful jacket," Halima translated. "It was my mother and father's last work together. You and your bright jacket will always have a special place in her heart. Its color is so happy that she forgets to be sad when she looks at it."

Sandra went to look for her checkbook.

"This jacket is coming with hefty strings attached to it," she said to Ken on her way out of the kitchen.

"Not a willing player in their little drama, huh?"

Sandra shook her head. That's not what she meant. "It's going to end up hanging in my closet because I won't be able to bring myself to wear it!"

Back in the entryway, Sandra took an invoice covered in Arabic script from Halima, who freed the jacket from her mother's quietly defiant hands.

More Arabic between the two women. Mrs. Al Tirhi dabbed her eyes.

"Please, my mother would like you to try on the jacket to make sure it fits, only, she says she will cry harder if she sees it on you." Halima tilted her head. "Can you go to a room with a mirror? We will wait here. Please understand."

Sandra avoided looking at Mrs. Al Tirhi. She took the jacket and walked into the main floor bathroom, the children and dog trailing in. She set her wallet on the bathroom counter and tore out a check. No pen. She'd fill it in later.

She slid her arms into the silk sleeves, like cool, soft water. A dream jacket. A jacket bound to be coveted. Sandra closed her eyes, imagining the smell of date palms and lush greenery. She heard laughter and splashing children. Something trickled far away. She had donned an oasis.

She opened her eyes and saw her boy playing with water from the faucet. She frowned and flicked the spigot off, disoriented by the mirage evaporating in her mind. There had been others, familiar and strange, at that ethereal pool.

"Ooh," goggled Sandra's thirteen-year-old. "You look like a queen."

"A golden jacket," enthused her son. "You could do magic in it!"

"You must be glad to finally have it," noted the intuitive-as-usual middle girl. "Is that the lady who made it?"

Sandra saw herself pause in the mirror, her shoulders rising and falling in a world-weary sigh. Explaining to the kids how things end, how devotion and business intertwine, how artistry in one person's hands can happen from another's prompt was so complicated. She looked at the children watching her in the mirror and appreciated the odd little lull in her house, as seven people and a dog stopped thinking, scheming, reacting, and simply waited.

"That lady and her husband made it, although I don't think he saw it finished." And to herself—I just realized, I don't know Mrs. Al Tirhi's first name.

Sandra took off the jacket. Logically, yes, it was hers, but emotionally it might never be. Her lovely life seldom demanded she give things up. She thought of Mr. Al Tirhi's knowing fingers. He had spent a lifetime dressing and undressing women while making love to just one. She could be as gallant. She could give the jacket back. The trick would be getting Mrs. Al Tirhi to accept what they both wanted.

Sandra strained to think of what words would convince Mrs. Al Tirhi that she, Sandra, valued a shared piece of art and memory enough to give it away. Her focus grew more fevered: what if Sarah and Hagar had woven their lives and the lives of their children into a virtuous — not vicious — cycle with the right words?

She put her check back into her wallet, spying a creased white business card and its bullish motto, "Nothing Is Impossible". While she might not agree with the late Mr. Al Tirhi's slogan, and while it wasn't on her head to right an ancient familial banishment, she had an opening here. To make amends, to mend, possibly even to share. Wry thoughts sprang up in Sandra's mind: split the jacket, like a time-share condo, like joint custody, like the way she and her sisters had once borrowed from each other's closets! Sole possession seemed like such an artifact of history. She emerged from the bathroom, jacket over her arm.

"Please," Sandra addressed her visitors, sweeping an arm towards the kitchen table. "Come sit down." She put the kettle on and generously spooned sugar into teacups, peppermint tea the way she knew Arabs and Jews drank it in the Old City, impossibly sweet.

Alley-Oop

Like the keeper of an oral tradition, my neighbor to the north, Glenn, a retired Boeing engineer, informed me the first week in our new house that alley residents fill potholes around their section of the alley with their own bags of stones and dirt. Alley residents clean up after their dogs. They avoid contacting the city to cut tree branches or complain about leftover garbage.

He looked over his glasses at me when I asked why and turned his hands out and up. None of the other alley residents I asked remembers or knows why. There are no old timers left to tell us why this city-owned ribbon of dirt has become an autonomous region for those who live along it. The ones who instructed Glenn moved away long ago.

Lined with a faded white fence from the 1970s, the alley, in summer, is eight blocks of loopy, verdant overhang — a coiling green tunnel, a haven for hummingbirds, dog walkers, and small boys.

My twins take branches and run them against the fence, producing a delicious kut-kut-kut sound, not unlike their mother's snores. I usually sleep in the guest room with earplugs — that's how loud my wife Celeste snores in the bedroom next door. As a stay-at-home-dad, I grab naps when Arthur and Benny go to preschool to make up for the sleep her snoring interrupts.

Except for the garbage and recycling trucks, which thunder through on Tuesday mornings, vehicles in the alley are rare. It's a safe place for the kids to play, like a long, extra backyard. Our Shelties chase squirrels and cats because, I am sure, racing the alley is the happiest thing they can do.

Fluff-balls with melt-your-heart brown eyes, the dogs stick their twitchy black noses through worn places in the fence. Tails and hind ends gyrate until some hidden signal sends them racing. Tha-wocketa, tha-wocketa, tha-wocketa, the sound of eight canine legs coming full tilt down the alley. They are riderless racehorses, ears and neck fluff flattened by their speed.

Glenn from next door comes walking out his back gateway, sporting a sly smile.

"I just saw two speeding bullets go by. Bet they were going twenty miles an hour." He tells me what a shame Washington State doesn't allow dog racing.

"Oregon does," he says. "That's why I got the camper bus." He jerks his thumb back in the direction of his huge open garage which abuts the alley. He scrunches his forehead, lowers his eyelids, a silent question on his face: *Can you keep a secret?*

"Birdie thinks I'm only going fishing. I got a regular spot in western Oregon along the Umpqua River. Besides, she doesn't like to leave her chickens."

"Do you bet?"

"You bet. Come with me some time. You're around the house a lot." Glenn's a bit of a meddler, I think. He sure seems to know everyone's business.

◇◇◇◇◇◇◇◇◇◇◇◇◇◇◇◇◇◇

I'm taking out recycling one Monday evening before Tuesday's garbage truck rodeo. The dogs whip past me, setting up the familiar racehorse cadence. I watch them tear south, which is how I first meet the Frenchwoman down the alley. She is loading her girls into the car. She screams, "*Mon Dieu!*" The dogs wheel around and scramble back, distracted by the woman and her whimpering daughters, maybe seven- or eight- or nine-years old.

"Who-ze dohgs arh deeze?" she yells at me. I try for a convincing French shrug. Who knows? My lower lip and chin form a giant upside-down U. To my surprise, this pacifies her. She smiles, nods her head at me and pushes the girls into the car, backing out roughly to the alley's southern entrance and onto the street.

I have already met her husband, Serge, and formed the opinion that he is a bully. One Tuesday afternoon I was in the alley gathering the garbage and recycling containers strewn about by the careless collectors. Parade-martial style, Serge came out of his back driveway, escorting his two daughters to a karate lesson. The girls wore white tunics and pants with orange belts. I saw him kick one in her behind, leaving a winking gray smudge as she quickened her steps to avoid a second kick. They hurried north, until they disappeared into the elementary school in front of which the alley ends.

In winter, the alley became deserted and sullen with its loss of leafy shelter. Once, I dashed out to the garbage in a downpour and startled two ducks dabbling in one of the bigger puddles.

As the days grew warmer, the alley again became a neighborhood hub. Glenn was in his backyard trimming bushes or chatting with alley residents. We heard Birdie— *Chicken Lady*—my boys called her, cooing over her caged biddies. She not only sounded like a chicken, she looked like a chicken with her feathery white hair and darting brown eyes. She shooed "the girls" aside and waved my boys over.

Arthur and Benny carefully cradled eggs she gave them in their little hands. Ever so slowly, they put one foot in front of another, heel to toe, heel to toe, until they reached our refrigerator, bursting back outside at full boy speed.

Rodney and Bliss, our neighbors to the south, sat on their back patio and drank with friends. Rodney sauntered out to the alley to drop a few champagne bottles into a recycling bin. They drank really good stuff. With two kids in college no less. Rodney spoke to Serge's wife in French.

One Saturday, I'd put a whiffle ball on a stand-up support for Arthur and Benny. They swung, missed and scrambled for the ball. Serge and Glenn were chatting. Glenn motioned me down to them.

"Do you know Serge?" Glenn asked. "He could verify how fast those doggies run." I stuck out my hand, "Sure, we've met." Serge gave me a shake that came close to hurting. I wondered about the state patrol car parked in his driveway.

"So long as they're going more than fifteen miles per hour," Serge said, walking over to the cruiser and opening the front passenger door.

He came back with a proud grin and a gray gun-like piece of equipment.

"Falcon hand-held radar." He pointed it at me. I learned that, yes, Serge was an officer with the state patrol.

Serge said he had an idea and went into his house. Returning, he stood in his driveway, about one hundred yards south of my place. His girls stood a few feet behind him. He told Arthur and Benny to take the Shelties back to our driveway and hold them until he shot his small silver gun, a starter's gun —more for impressing the kids than for the dogs, in my view. He waved his arm and pointed the gun up. My boys let go of the dogs at the shot, but the Shelties only turned in nervous circles.

"They need a squirrel to chase," Glenn said.

Arthur ran into our house and came out with a gray stuffed rhinoceros, which we attached with a string onto the back of my old ten-speed. I pedaled wildly and the rhinoceros bounced up over rocks and dirt, which did the trick. The dogs came after it. Two snouts clamped down on the rhinoceros and ripped it free of its tether. As if joined at the jaw, the dogs galloped back up the alley, neither letting go of the rhinoceros.

"Need something faster than a bike," Glenn fretted.

Walkie-talkies got involved, with someone stationed at each end of the alley. Serge used his radar. Arthur and Benny raided the stuffed animal collection that got added to whenever their mother returned from a trip. Glenn started talking about odds on the dogs and wanted to set up time trials.

I shared few of these details with Celeste. She traveled so much I hardly saw her anyway. I had my neighborhood world. She had her loaded global clients.

Five years ago, she'd just been made a partner in her firm when the ultrasound sent shock waves through her office and our relationship.

"She's having twins at forty-two!"

Upon learning our news, a number of long-time friends and co-workers of Celeste's asked if we'd had, you know, some *help*? We'd been married and childless for twelve years, after all.

I had smiled lasciviously, "A nice Merlot, some Belgian chocolates."

Celeste went back to work six months after Benny and Arthur were born, and I've been home with them for four years now. We like our arrangement well enough, although when asked what it is I do, I jokingly say I'm a personal assistant to three very busy people.

◇◇◇◇◇◇◇◇◇◇◇◇◇◇◇◇◇◇

Our second July in the house and a year after Glenn first raised the possibility of a road trip, the boys and I went to a car show. Celeste had been in London all week, so when I saw the pale green Vespa…there might have been some wanting to even things out. The boys and I fit nicely on the long black seat. Benny clinched the deal by saying, "The dogs will love to chase this." The Vespa was scheduled to be delivered.

I bought three helmets and we wore them in the car on the ride home, singing at the top of our lungs, "Oh, the boys on the scooter go vroom, vroom, vroom." When we got home, Arthur and Benny ran next door to tell Glenn.

Glenn suggested a weekend afternoon dog race. This conversation came about in Serge's driveway, in spite of his wife's dark utterances. She thought it was a really bad idea. "We're not hurting the dogs," we men remonstrated.

"Dogs like to run, live to run." "At the end of each race, we'll give the dogs a treat."

"*C'est pas bien.*" It's not good, said the wife, Katrine. Serge looked like he wanted to kick her. She pushed her brown bangs out of her face, her sleeveless top revealing startlingly dark hair under her arms. I glanced down. The unshaved hair on her legs looked silky.

Bliss and Rodney leaned over their fence. They had been working in the garden and were taking a champagne break.

"*A vôtre santé,*" they called to Katrine, who bobbed her head.

Katrine, I found out, is a legal assistant for a law firm that does business with French and American companies. She met Serge when he testified in one of their cases. I wondered if I should mention that my wife is a corporate tax lawyer. I didn't.

The Vespa-dog race idea hung in the air, though no date was set. Summer started to get away from us because, suddenly, it was August.

Serge had signs put up at each of the alley's entrances, "Greetings, This is a Crime Watch Neighborhood." I looked at the giant sideways eye on the sign, like something you would see on an Egyptian tomb. Who needs this? I am aggrieved that the posting of these signs never got discussed with any neighbors — me for instance — and voted on.

When I brought it up with Glenn, his response was that Serge knows how to get things done, and when are we going to Oregon? Glenn wanted someone to share the driving with him. The old farts he used to go with don't want to drive that far any more.

"We'll take the twins and go south for a week before their school starts," he proposed. Glenn first wanted to fish on the Umpqua and on the way home swing by the dog track at Portland Meadows.

Celeste lifted an eyebrow and reluctantly agreed to the plan (I didn't mention the dog racing part) so long as the boys never took off their life preservers. Since Celeste would be in New York while we drove to Oregon, Glenn suggested we take the dogs with us. Arthur and Benny cheered madly. I didn't see how this would possibly be a vacation for me.

◇◇◇◇◇◇◇◇◇◇◇◇◇◇◇◇◇◇◇◇

The day before our departure, Arthur and Benny clamber in and out of Glenn's monster camper bus, counting the rooms. Celeste stows their favorite snack foods in the rig's kitchen cabinets. Glenn and I attach my scooter to the over-sized camper's huge rear fender.

Early the next morning, two sleepy boys say good-bye to Mommy while she hands me lip salve and wet wipes. I listen with half an ear as Celeste goes through her itinerary with me, again. She leaves for New York shortly, isn't sure when she will return. We can hear Glenn maneuvering the bus into the alley. A few minutes later he comes through our back door.

"Remember to take the dogs' water and food bowls." Celeste kicks at the plastic bowls on the floor, the loftiness in her voice nearly dripping out of her extended pointer finger. "Wish I could go with you. Have a good time," she says magnanimously, when the cab driver knocks on the front door.

Frenzied pecks and she is gone. Glenn, taking it all in, looks as if he has witnessed a miracle: deliverance, finally, from the ballbasher! He reminds me that he first brought up the idea of an expedition a year ago. Ah, but the devil often hitches a ride with salvation.

We lurch down the alley and curve slowly onto the main street, disgusting black smoke spitting out the bus' back end. The boys bounce on the cushioned benches and send their action figures into the air before crashing them into the dining table.

Glenn and I are commenting on Interstate-5's sparse south-bound traffic when the door to one of the bus's back bedrooms opens. It's Katrine, purple and yellow bruises around her right eye, and two silent girls.

I stare up into the rearview mirror. "We have some stowaways."

"Not exactly." Glenn gives me a thin smile, the old goat. "Runaways."

Katrine shrugs, embarrassed.

"My husband is a police officer. He could find me if I tried to get away by myself, so we get away this way. You won't pour the beans?"

"Did you know about this?" I ask Glenn, incredulous.

"I suggested it."

Forget fishing and dog racing and tootling around on the scooter. I have fallen in with thieves. Scenarios flood my brain: Serge bullying Celeste or Birdie into revealing our whereabouts, Celeste getting jealous, Serge getting jealous, Serge beating me up, Celeste taking up with Serge. Then I remember that Celeste is on her way to New York, which is why the boys, dogs, and I are with Glenn.

"This may not look good," I whine. "My wife thought I was going on a good ol' boys' fishing trip."

The four kids have found a pack of Glenn's cards and are playing Go Fish. Katrine kneels on the floor between Glenn and me and pushes her bangs out of her face. I catch a glimpse and an acrid whiff of her hairy armpits.

"Did Serge hit you?" I ask softly.

"For ze last time."

I grimly grip the big steering wheel with both hands, checking the side mirrors for any whirling red lights. Katrine lowers her arms across her chest and gently laments Glenn's no-smoking rule. She pulls back into the interior of the bus when she sees a state patrol car. This makes me very nervous.

Hours later, the setting sun turns everything glinty orange along the rutted road into the trailer park. In contrast, the Lower Umpqua River, shaded by thick alders, is opalescent green, a cloudy gem. Dozens of peanut-shaped sand bars rise out of the shallow water, beckoning the kids to wade and leap from miniature "island" to "island."

Imaginary fingers are squeezing my eyes into my head. My real fingers are numb. My body hums at the same frequency as the camper bus' engine. Turns out Glenn preferred to point at signs and wave towards exits than actually drive the behemoth.

The children splash and squeal while Glenn pulls out his grill. Enough feeling returns to my body for me to offer to get cold beer at the grocery we passed a few miles back. I head to the camper bus to untie the Vespa, pocket full of cash Glenn has pushed at me.

"I'll watch the kids. Take Katrine," Glenn presses. I put my cell phone in the bus to avoid answering any unwanted calls and invite her to get behind me.

Surprise flushes my face when she wraps her arms about my middle without hesitation. My stomach, heart, head, and crotch are all on alert. Once out of the trailer park, she lays her head against my back.

"*Comme ma jeunesse*, like when I was young," she shouts into my neck. I imagine carefree laughter bouncing off Parisian walls, youths racing over ancient cobblestones.

She lived along Rue Gay-Lussac in Paris, Katrine tells me, when we get off the scooter. She and her sister put pillows over their ears to shut out the late-night motorbikes — until her boyfriend got one and regularly waited for her to clamber down the fire escape.

I am courteous, while pretending to concentrate on the shop's incredibly small beer and wine selection. I don't want to be seen as extending anything other than a sympathetic ear, which is still listening for the wap-wap-wap of a police helicopter.

The next morning stretches out like a laundry-line of sundresses: cheery and eager to be worn someplace fun. Glenn gets up early and returns with fish to fry. Katrine has everyone sit down together and makes us all a little crazy with her hovering and fussing around the table. At this meal and at all subsequent ones, she has folded the paper napkins into something amusing —bishop's hats, candles, frogs. The kids eat mostly popsicles. By the second evening in the campground, I stop expecting a SWAT team to surround us at any minute.

The third evening, after we put the kids to bed, the three adults sit around Glenn's fire, sipping the French wine Katrine insisted we buy at the grocery. Katrine keeps touching my hand or my forearm when she makes a point. Glenn tells me to put out the fire properly before I go to bed. He's turning in.

I jump up and am about to say, me too. He gives me his can-you-keep-a-secret face: *You gonna take charge here, son?* I put another log on the fire and reflect that my forte has always been in meeting other people's needs.

Four idyllic days go by. Each morning after Katrine finishes with her girls' hair, she takes out a second brush, bought at the trailer park office store, and brushes the dogs meticulously. They droop with adoration for her.

Hard to say who is happier in our little camp. My boys brandish sticks in endless fantasy games. The dogs run and chase each other, canine counterparts to the boys. Katrine's girls have threaded dandelions together to create sunny crowns and necklaces. The boys call them Nico and Baba, short for Nicolette and Babette, names they can't say. Glenn asks the kids to call him Grandpa. He and Birdie await their first grandchild in December. Surely now is a good opportunity to practice being one, he says grandly.

Katrine and I get away for a daily expedition on the scooter, through backwater hamlets and stretches of pastures full of cows, even an odd llama. I appreciate femininity in a new way. A long-forgotten self-possession returns with a woman's arms wrapped unpretentiously around my waist. I think back to nights when Celeste and I held each other in similar fashion. It's more fun at 40 miles per hour. I guess Celeste has a tendency to be hard-bitten. Not that I don't respect her calling a spade a shovel now and then.

Glenn approaches me the last evening. With a few phone calls, he has cooked up a plan for Katrine. I shake my head at this old man and his penchant for planning other people's lives without their input, without my input anyway. I want no part in their scheme, the potential for discovery is too great.

Kids in bed, Katrine walks with me along the river to a secluded, grassy bank we found the first day. We roll out a sleeping bag and she suggests sex *en plein air*. Who can say no to a breathy French accent and a woman who doesn't wear underpants? I return to the campground committed.

We pull into the parking garage of Portland International Airport the next afternoon. Glenn thinks his presence will look suspicious so he says good-bye to Katrine and the girls in the bus.

The rest of us throng around the United Airlines desk. From Portland, there is a flight to New York connecting with Air France, and back to the bosom of Katrine's Parisian family. The girls, minors, are on her passport. The way is paved.

Katrine leans sadly on the ticket counter and speaks in a low voice about her dying mother. I play the resolute husband who will stay behind to watch the boys who are too young to travel so far. Just the girls will go with their mother.

I put my arm solicitously around her shoulders, as Katrine closes her eyes. The United Airlines clerk tears up herself and offers condolences, asks about baggage. "No time to pack," I jump in briskly, "we came straight to the airport."

Katrine flashes her credit card. I kiss her gently on the right temple and need to lean my groin into the ticket counter because of what the smell of her skin is doing to me. Tickets are handed over and we trudge away. No calls to security, no armed hunk gets in our faces. Katrine and the girls are free to go and the boys and I are, truthfully, heavy-hearted.

"When will you be back, honey?" I ask. Playacting has drained into real living, a rich confusion I am sorry to shed.

"*Je ne suis pas,* I don't know, *mon coeur.*"

I alley-oop Baba and Nico into the air. Katrine wipes her eyes and ruffles Arthur and Benny's hair. She comes close to me. "*Merci,* thank you for everything," and, mouth-to-mouth, we cause determined travelers to swerve around our passionate French kiss. Cue the accordionist.

The boys and I wave until we can no longer see Katrine and her girls walking down the airport corridor.

When we return to the bus, Glenn is dozing in the driver's seat. I tell him to go lie down in back. I'll drive. He doesn't argue—we've tuckered him out.

We're a few miles from crossing the Columbia River, coming into Washington State, when I see the sign. The dogs' legs swing forward and back in slow motion outside the coliseum-like entrance to Portland Meadows.

I listen to Glenn's rhythmic gurgles. Arthur is crashed on one of the day beds. Benny's eyes are at half-mast. The decision to keep driving is an easy one.

"Look, Benny," I whisper, and point off to the right. Benny, my philosopher, says sleepily, "I feel sorry for him, running and running and staying in the same place."

I tell Benny the long drive ahead will go faster if he puts his head down next to Arthur's. He acquiesces with a slow plop, giving me nearly three hours to listen to the voice in my head and the three sets of snores wafting through the bus. I fish out my cell phone and leave a message for Celeste about our expected arrival time.

Everyone stirs awake as I decelerate off the freeway ramp and head toward our neighborhood. Expecting to coast down the alley, I am unable to even enter it, due to a thicket of orange and white barricades at its south entrance. Glenn and I look at the barricades, perplexed, and then we look up.

"Oh, my God," we say together. The trees on both sides of the alley have been cut clean away. No more shade or droop. Everyone's backyard is visible.

"That mean son-of-a-bitch," Glenn mutters.

"Serge?" A claw of fear tightens around my stomach.

I get out of the bus to move the signs to the side of the alley entrance. We chug into Glenn's backyard bus port and pile out to survey the alley. The dogs pha-lump, pha-lump down the bus stairs and stand around, puzzled, as if trying to put a doggie finger on what is different. The alley is awash in small branches and leaves.

Celeste fills me in on what she knows. I am relieved she's talking so matter-of-factly about everything and, strangely, I find myself comforted to be back to her no-nonsense view of the world.

She tells me Serge decided Katrine and the girls must have been kidnapped out the back bedroom window, an easy task considering the cover all the alley trees provided. (Katrine had told me she'd left open the girls' bedroom window and had dragged a ladder underneath it to create confusion.)

"Public safety at stake," Serge had roared. Through his connections with the city, a work crew was dispatched to butcher the alley's trees.

"Just happened yesterday," Celeste frowns. "I can see Serge being worried or mad, but to take it out on all of us?"

"I guess that's how Serge is," I shrug. Celeste looks at me appraisingly. She's a lawyer. She knows better than to ask questions that might produce incriminating evidence.

There's nothing for the twins to eat at home, and I offer to make a store run on the Vespa.

"Come for a ride with me," I urge. "We can leave the boys with Glenn and Birdie." Celeste sighs, as if calculating the risks of saying no. I reach for her hand and try to imitate Peter Sellers, "Buht aye inseest!" You have to push back sometimes.

"If I can wear the helmet."

"Moment." I pirouette out the back door to go get it and to apprise Glenn. Celeste looks cute in a helmet. We putter down the alley — potholes and odiferous garbage cans giving way, in my mind, to cobblestones and the smell of café-au-lait. I fishtail out of the alley and speed down the street, Celeste screeching, "Slow down."

"Wrap your arms around me, baby," I yell back, and she does.

Buried Alive in Belgrade

Red roses sure can gum up a girl's straight thinking. Brad gave me a dozen twenty years ago and now he's gone and done it again. This time I agree to go for coffee. Last time, I agreed to go camping, unaware it was a form of foreplay in Montana. In Western Washington, we start at café tables, not with tents.

The first roses showed up in 1988 on the second night of a two-week engagement in Butte. The bouquet basked on stage atop a bar stool. The Blue Streaks lead singer sprang forward, only to turn in surprise. "They're for Ellie."

The banjo player whistled. "A secret admirer." Not so secret. The card attached to the flowers was signed: "I like your fiddling, Brad T."

I searched the crowd. No guy with a give-away smile.

To sustained hollers from stomping, table-banging beer drinkers, we closed the second set with a Cajun barnburner. I felt let down that no Brad T. had come forward, and shuffled into the wings to set my violin in its stand. I clomped down worn wooden steps at the side of the stage and into a well-filled jean jacket.

"I like your fiddlin,'" the jacket said. The initials "BT" on his belt buckle made my knees go gooey. A strong arm supported me as I hopped down to the final stair and onto the dance floor. He was a young version of the Marlboro man: Stetson, cowboy shirt, bolo tie, worn jeans, and cowboy boots. A sheathed knife was strapped to his belt. No good German-Jewish American girl could have sanely envisioned this scenario. "You want to talk to *me?*"

His extended right hand was sun-warmed forbidden fruit. "Brad Thyssen. Let me buy you a drink."

I was introduced to Brad's tablemates, Earl and Charlie. Genial chatter filled the break.

"What do you do when you're done?" Brad asked when the band leader signaled me back for the final set.

"We go across the street to the M and M Diner and then to bed." Saying the word bed made me blush, and babble for cover. "Three to a hotel room to save money."

Brad came back the next night to invite the band to his place, a wheat ranch inherited from a father dead from lung cancer. His mother had moved to town. To my citified view of the world, Brad hardly seemed old enough to be running a ranch. He gave me a good-ole-boy chin chuck. "Life toughens you fast out here, darlin.' You live hard and you party hard."

After we finished at the bar, the band and Brad's many friends caravaned to his place in Belgrade, outside Butte. We jammed and drank until our eyelids quit taking orders from our brains and fell shut.

Fully clothed, Brad and I flopped onto his bed for what seemed a minute before he was rousing me to follow him through the scattered sleepers. He threw a jacket over my shoulders and led me outside to a barn. From one of the stalls, he walked out backwards with a shiny red motor bike, his generation's horse. I wrapped my arms around his middle and we puttered off.

Furry, white rumps flashed in the slurry lavender light as we crested a small hill. Brad sped up, but the antelopes easily careened away over the next ridge. "Don't have my gun. Too lean to eat anyway."

"You *shoot* them?"

"Silly city girl." Brad shut down the bike. I slid off the back, and Brad dismounted with a flung leg over the bike. Dawn started as a yellow-gray rose before reshaping itself into mighty beams of light, humming with portent. My body vibrated from lack of sleep and what surely were unheard frequencies.

"Anybody can see a sunset. It's a select few that're up for a sunrise." Brad hugged my waist. "Just you and me and 4,600 acres of wheat." I drew a long, showy inhalation through my nose: a toasty smell — homey — like a newly opened box of breakfast cereal.

I extended my arms towards the sun in obeisance. "Don't you wonder how such a show was set in motion?" I dropped my arms. The Fine Arts major wished to impress. "A scene like this challenges the mind the way great art challenges the mind."

"It's great art, alright." Brad apparently wanted to prove my conversational equal. "God's art, you know — the sun, the moon, the stars."

My elitist crack, "How spatial," prompted him to wrap his other arm around me. "It *is* special, and you're a special young lady."

Uch, such cornball coquetry. His breath fogged my lips.

"I'm not so sure about this," I protested, very mildly.

"I can fix that." His mouth over mine, I tasted cigarettes and whiskey and grit and sour saliva, a Wild West kiss. His stubble scratched my cheek. "Let's go camping," Brad moaned.

∞∞∞∞∞∞∞∞∞∞∞∞∞∞

This afternoon, after an awkward hesitation, Brad takes my outstretched hand and yanks me into a hug no less rib-cracking than the ones he'd given me two decades earlier. My God, he still smells of pungent straw bales and sun-dried denim. Not what you'd expect in a Seattle Starbucks. We tango over who will pay for the coffees and I give in. "Keep the change, darlin,'" Brad tells a green-apron-clad girl.

We sit and sip and study each other. He ventures first. "You look great, a little more exotic."

"It's the Jewfro." I toss the once-straightened kinky curls. "I'm really Jewish now." I tense for his reaction.

Brad frowns. "What were you when I met you?"

"I wasn't practicing then."

"Well, ya couldda fooled me. You sounded great."

I pat his hand, bemused. "I'm not who I was."

"Who is? I quit smoking."

∞∞∞∞∞∞∞∞∞∞∞∞∞∞

The day after Brad's party, four of us had pitched pup tents above a winsome river, somewhere north of Belgrade. The Blue Streaks' Thursday-through-Sunday-night booking left me three free days before needing to reconnect with the band back in Butte.

While Brad and Charlie fished, Earl and I had pulled out a propane stove from under cases of beer in the back of Brad's pickup. The menu took shape: canned beans, chips, beer and, maybe, fish. From the length of Brad and Charlie's absence, the fish weren't as hungry as we were.

"Brad's so hung up on you he couldn't pour piss out of a boot if the instructions were on the heel." Earl leered at me over a third beer.

In Montana that must mean you're really in love, I thought, though you'd have to be pretty dumb to be peeing in your boot in the first place. I didn't encourage Earl with a response.

The guys had been making up yarns all day, seeing how much they could get over on me: local reindeer with bells growing in the scruff of their necks, furry critters with shorter legs on the summit side of their bodies to aid in winding up hills. I'd laughed uneasily with them when they poked each other and me.

I felt less and less sure about this camping trip with three men, no telephones, and no idea where to go or how to get away if I needed to. "There must be nice girls in your town."

Earl held off lighting a cigarette and scoffed. "He's tried the local girls. Brad's hard to please. Got a reputation of being too big for his britches."

I left that alone and suggested, "He's got aspirations beyond survival."

Earl look stumped. Finally, I'd made him feel inferior, and he didn't know how. Hostility Jewish-style.

Dinner was canned beans and beer and a fish. After a large bonfire and more beer, Earl and Charlie stumbled off to their tents.

"There ain't but one tent left," Brad beckoned. Inside, despite the total blackness, we had no trouble finding the parts that needed to be found. I slid my hands into my back pocket and pulled out a condom. Not such a silly city girl.

Brad lessened his rocking. "Not now."

"If not now, when?" Apologies to Rabbi Hillel the Elder.

"It probably won't fit," he grumped, fumbling with the latex. In the vast expanse of the tent, the condom got lost, and so did my composure. I pushed away. "You dragged me out to the wilderness for sex and inferior food so you could boast about your exploits once I'm gone."

"My whats?"

Dolt! "Besides, I can't afford to get pregnant."

Brad stopped bucking and cradled my face in his hands. "Quit the band. I'm a rancher. You can live offa me." Raising a passel of Brad babies on a wheat farm was a rare and confounding possibility. It appealed to the earthmother in me, who nurtured a pea-patch in the city, who wistfully watched the dobro player's wife secure their infant to her massive breasts.

"Too drastic a lifestyle change," I muttered, followed by unexpected tears of confusion. With exquisite lightness, Brad's calloused thumbs brushed underneath my eyes. Only an insecure fool like me would have underestimated such depth.

In heavy morning rain, we packed up and returned to Brad's ranch. Earl and Charlie got into their respective pickups. I dithered: back to Butte early to hang out with the band before the next round of shows or stay at Brad's place? My curiosity, Brad's coaxing, and the lure of an unencumbered fling trumped my *shpilkes*, restlessness. I set my violin underneath Brad's overflowing kitchen table.

Brad's hired men arrived, talking harvesters and mechanics and crop prices. Swiftly relegated to an observer, I wandered away to look at a huge horse pasture and to scrutinize my intentions. Dallying with Brad's heart was unkind. I had no business entertaining the notion that I could thrive in such an unpeopled place. Unlike Brad, I was spooked by the land's enormity, at the thought of subduing animals and people and nature on such a grand scale. A breeze carried the smell of the men's cigarettes, the sound of their hacking and their low laughter.

Fat raindrops sent me scurrying into the house. Bored, I began collecting beer bottles. The kitchen counters were still post-party gross and sticky. I washed down the counters, cleared dishes out of the sink. Cleaning Brad's place was different from slogging through my own dross in a spare Seattle apartment. With repeated scrubbing, the linoleum had turned shiny and the windows transparent by the time Brad stuck his head in the kitchen door. He let out an admiring whistle.

"Take off your boots," I yelled. In socks, he slid across the smooth vinyl and tackled me with a breath-stopping embrace and a sloppy kiss. Choreplay.

"Too bad we got company." Brad nibbled my ear lobe. "Later, okay?" He took several wrapped packages of meat out of the refrigerator. "Grill's already fired up."

The guys could have been High Priests in the ancient temple for all the care and discussion that went into the next hour of ritual roasting. I listened to the men opine on seasonings, heat, number of times the meat should be turned, what the dang cow ate. More beer. More talk. The hired men were in no hurry and neither was Brad. My irritation at the way they kept on jawing got folded into the intricate shape of the napkin I placed on each plate. I laid the napkin flat, creased the left side over, flipped the napkin, folded from the right, tucked in the ends and stood it up: a Bishop's Hat. When we finally got around to sitting down, Brad and the hired men watched me take my napkin apart and set it in my lap before following suit, their shared glances saying, *Somethin' a little different here.*

It was late by the time they rose from the dinner table, their handshakes leaving my palm lightly lubricated from the greasy ribs we'd eaten. I stood at the kitchen sink, up to my elbows in soapy lather, and, through an adjacent window, watched the men jostle each other and call back and forth, clearly reluctant to separate. Brad waved them off into the dark, rainy night and stayed outside smoking until the two trucks' rear red lights could no longer be seen snaking down the road.

I heard him close the front door and wondered at his hesitation, until the thunk of his boots being dropped in the entry way doused the jealous spark his prolonged goodbyes had generated in me. What a good man to remember about the floor.

We cozied up on a lumpy couch to view his family photo albums: the great-grandparents who came first; the grandparents who acquired more land; the parents whose health and disposition ended their term of stewardship prematurely; Brad and his older brother Robbie. Brad got the sturdy genes, Robbie the looks.

"Where is Robbie?"

"He's the smart one, went to medical school. He's finishing his residency at the UW."

"Seattle? Do you visit him?" This was cause for concern. Brad might show up and complicate the big-city relationship I had with a certain graduate school student.

"Robbie and I aren't close," Brad said. "We're really different."

We moved to the covered back porch with a bottle of Jack Daniels and my violin. The dreary evening seemed better served by Jewish folk tunes, bittersweet musical pleas. "Country Eastern," I joked, improvising in a minor mode.

"Uh, it's pretty," Brad said, unconvincingly. "I prefer Country Western."

I sang with an exaggerated twang. "Give me the roses while I live, learning to carry on. Useless are flowers that you give after the soul has gone." I gulped air. The weight of sky and endless hills made breathing a conscious effort. I could not imagine a lifetime of such suffocating solitude and silence. Whiskey gone, we wove our way to his bedroom.

"You'll think about it?" Brad asked in the morning.

No, I said inside my head. "I'll think about it."

◇◇◇◇◇◇◇◇◇◇◇◇◇◇◇◇◇◇◇◇

Brad is still tanned and charming. He flops one arm over the back of a chair and would probably put his feet up, too, if the coffee shop, catering to the doctors and divas between Seattle's Pill Hill and Capitol Hill, were less crowded. His sideburns have gone gray. Grooves radiating from the outside corners of his eyes attest to all the squinting he's done under sunny Montana skies. His ranch work has left its imprint on his appearance, on his character. A rancher looks and moves like a rancher; couldn't mistake Brad for anything else. He tells me he is a dying breed and I believe him. "Could use a little mouth-to-mouth resuscitation," he says with a hound-dog grin. He means for the other coffee drinkers, so very deep in self-important conversation, to hear.

I tell Brad I've moved many times since meeting him in Butte, exchanging bluegrass for the Klezmer sound of my European ancestors. I'm a single mother, after all, raising two teen-aged daughters within the nurturing confines of a synagogue community. There'd been no thought to venturing out of that gentle harness until his roses arrived at the *shul* where I work. I scan Brad's rural face, so different a countenance from the leather-and-black hipsters and harried, scrub-wearing hospital workers around us. "How on earth did you find me?"

"My brother's partner is—was—Jewish, and he tracked you down for me."

I sit very still, cautious of the conversation's direction.

"I never told you my brother was gay, did I? That's why I'm in Seattle. He lost his fight with AIDS last week." Brad clenches and unclenches his jaw. The rims of his eyes get pink and pinker. "For not having been around him much, it sure is hitting me hard."

I sink back into my chair. Hard to believe we were once young and marvelous. We've both acquired all these unwanted layers. I escaped Brad's life, only to carry around the weight of questionable choices made in other places. Twenty-four roses bookend so many life-changing years: a long-ago Montana encounter, faded youthful promise, the uncertain likelihood of future engagement. Brad looks sad and old and I feel a party to it. He is an eternity who wants to be a day.

"I'm sorry," I mumble, searching for a sympathetic reply, coming up with a vague version of something heard at services. " 'It's a holy thing to love what death touches…' Is there anything I can do?"

"Come visit me."

"No wife, no kids?"

"Had a few girlfriends here and there," he allows.

I zigzag, a rabbit eluding a pursuer, careful lest my line of questioning reveal more than I am ready to. "Whatever happened to Earl and Charlie?"

"Earl got drunk and drove down the wrong side of the freeway into a semi." I cringe, and feel a guilty twinge about having made him feel stupid. "Charlie's got a bunch of kids and a few ex-wives. I think he's in Missoula."

Brad pauses. "I really regret letting you leave, Ellie. I've thought of you a lot over the years." His sincerity cuts like a stiletto through my show of ambiguous romantic availability.

It's scary being honest. I lick my lips and say it. "The person I am now would have stayed." Jews weren't always wanderers, weren't always pulling up tent stakes. There is a thin, genetic strand of remembrance, of wanting to plant and sow, of harvesting barley and oranges in a sunny, ancient home. The bond to a land that courses through Brad once defined my people. I'm at a place in my life where I seek landedness, and love. Brad is drawn to my cultural expanse. He's still looking for a ranch wife with a world view.

Brad brightens. "Bring your girls. I won't give nothin' away about our past." Anything, I correct silently.

"You'll think about it?"

Yes, I say inside my head. "I'll think about it."

On my way home, I swing by the synagogue office for the roses. Their perfection taunts me, each fault-free bud neatly coiled atop a straight stalk. I want to shake the bouquet, make it frowzy.

From some ancient Reservoir of Being, a forbear whispers: whirl them. Why not? An Orthodox Jew swings a live chicken, a symbolic sacrifice, *shlog kapores,* in a circle above his head to free him of impurities at Yom Kippur. (The chicken is butchered and given to the poor.)

I raise the bouquet aloft in my backyard hoping no one will see this preposterous display, this release. I swing the roses around and around. For Brad's brother, Robbie, who died too soon. For my daughters who need a healthy father figure. For Brad, pressed by sky into the soil, deeper and deeper each day of each year. For me and my indecisions that became decisions.

Petals float down on the grass as if spatters of blood. The sullied roses better befit my life. Bedraggled beauty. Winded and satisfied, I place them in a vase.

Honest-to-God, there is a REI catalog for outdoor equipment in the mail that afternoon!

Home after softball turnout, my daughters Abby and Lena are intrigued at my interest in tents and by the buffeted bouquet. "Who gave you roses? What happened to them? What's today?" Questions I hear as: A new boyfriend? An apology from Dad? Did we forget your birthday?

What I want to say them is, *The rest of your life is a long time to regret something.* Only it comes out, "What do you think about a camping trip this summer?"

They recoil at this lunacy. I press on. "Hey, the Patriarchs and Matriarchs spent their whole lives in tents. We'd be reliving the past." The girls scurry by me for the refrigerator.

"You'll think about it?" I call after them. They groan from behind the opened refrigerator door and rummage protractedly through its shelves. When they finally exit the kitchen, I am left examining the camping catalog and my motives for such an excursion. I flip through the pages again and again, seeking some unnamed, unformed—ultimately unknowable—revelation in the snugness of a tied tent flap, the strength of waterproof outer wear. Like sojourners before me, I hope to find the most enduring even in the most temporary.

Lady-in-Waiting

When she'd opened the front door that sunny spring afternoon, Lenni's nurturing side had trumped her nervousness. "Let me make you a cup of tea," she'd said impulsively to the forensic psychologist—a moment of civility, a turning point even, in a pitched custody battle.

The psychologist had landed on one of the tall kitchen stools by the breakfast bar, from which Lenni's girls, Rachel and Julie, could be seen in the backyard. The boy, Shane, was on the tire swing. Teacups in hand, the two women moved outside to a patio table, the scene, in Lenni's mind, like a visit between next-door neighbors. The psychologist sniffed a rose and gave a faint smile, the first and only one that afternoon. Nature as transformative agent, Lenni had confirmed silently, hearing in her head the lines of the prayer she'd started memorizing.

May it be my custom to go outdoors each day
Among the trees and grass.

The psychologist's questions for Lenni had started with one not on the form. "Who's the gardener?"

Lenni pointed to herself. After keeping company with insensate books all day, she needed the fleshy feel of stalk and leaf to clear her mind of sages past, prophetesses present. "I'm the librarian for the Jewish Studies Department only by day," she'd said with a pleased smile.

◇◇◇◇◇◇◇◇◇◇◇◇◇◇◇◇◇◇◇◇◇

Lenni thought of that spring interview as she now watched the forensic psychologist, voice like flaking skin, respond to one of the attorneys. "Randall Sidoine's partner, Lenni Mackoff, presented as nondefensive, appropriately concerned, and committed to fostering his son Shane's emotional and academic success."

The judge told the psychologist to speak louder.

"Most notable during the one-hour interview was a lack of anger or vindictiveness common for involved parties in high-conflict custody matters. Ms. Mackoff made few comments regarding Shane's mother during the interview and focused her observations and concerns on the child." The forensic psychologist might have been reading a grocery list for all her seeming interest in the subject — a professional tedium from years of stewarding opposing parents, Lenni figured. Only prophets raged more loudly as the years progressed, treating minor intransigence as cosmic injustice.

"All children present during the parent-child observations were comfortable with Ms. Mackoff and sought her out for conversation and attention. She was gently supportive, flexible, and child-centered in her interactions with them."

If there were no more questions, the judge said, the forensic psychologist could step down. And step out of Shane's life, Lenni mused. No wonder the woman needed to be detached — her window of time with them was finite and she knew it. Parents, on the other hand, were dumbfounded at the prospect of having a child removed from their lives. Or taken from them by death. Lenni shuddered and thought of the small book on her bed table. She had meant to put it out on the library shelves. Instead, she had brought it home. Each night she pored over the 18th century lines written by the Ukrainian rabbi, Nachman of Bratslav, who poured his personal anguish into majestic leaps.

God, grant me the ability to be alone.

She had written her response to him on the only paper handy, a bank receipt, and folded it carefully into her wallet. *Ego is no match against the enormousness of eternity.*

The last witness was called, Shane's elementary school principal. The principal answered the attorney's questions with great gravity, as if reluctant to release his words into the courtroom.

"Yes," the principal intoned. "On numerous occasions, Shane Sidoine's mother, Crystal Waltham, told me she should, and I quote, 'Just go home and kill myself.'"

The courtroom shrank as the participants sucked in air, Crystal Waltham gasping loudest of all. She glared into space and muttered.

The judge called the two attorneys to the bench.

Crystal used the pause to look in Lenni's direction. Crystal tilted her head back and mouthed "bitch" into the air, the word drifting down to the gray tile floor like dying tails of fireworks. Lenni looked into her lap, pressed her hands together hard.

Not long after the trial, Randall and Lenni's attorney called them with the good news. The judge had given them full custody. Shane could visit his mother two weekends a month. Crystal's bizarre behavior was endangering the boy's mental health, the judge had ruled. Besides, Crystal could never get him to school on time.

Randall wept quietly, spent emotionally and financially. Lenni stroked the back of his neck. She closed her eyes, offered up a silent prayer of thanks. There was still half the summer left. She thought of garden tools to buy Shane and of worms and black dirt: the stuff of little boys.

A week later, Shane and his first box came to their house for good. He stood in the entry, a scrawny six-year-old, not making eye contact with anyone. He called Lenni "her" in withering tones. Lenni's girls escorted him up the stairs to show him his cleaned and decorated room. He responded by slamming the bedroom door, leaving Rachel, Julie, Lenni, and Randall wide-eyed and silent.

The first morning of Shane officially living at their house, Lenni walked into the kitchen to see him standing on a chair pushed against the counter. Hugging a cereal box to his chest, he placed a flake at a time into his mouth.

Lenni was surprised. "Shane, we sit down at the table with a bowl and a spoon," she said guiding him, hand on his shoulder, to the table. Shane looked straight ahead and upended the box, dumping cereal onto the table and the floor. Lenni steered him to the broom closet with a firm hold on his upper arm. "You'll need to clean your mess," she said. He broke away and ran outside, calling her names not before heard in the Sidoine-Mackoff household. She wondered if Shane thought she meant to shut him up in the closet.

"He's used to survival mode," Randall later told her, after hearing about the incident. "Go easy on him. He doesn't know his mother is nuts. Life wasn't good or bad, it just was. He'll eventually learn the difference."

Lenni simplified her requests, used fewer words. "Look into my face. What's the magic word? Please clear your place. Please speak up. Say goodbye when you leave. Say thank you."

Words of gratitude wake up your soul to goodness. She tore off the corner of the calendar where she had scribbled her thought and put the scrap in her apron pocket.

The next day, a search for her hair dryer ended in Shane's room. He was building a hovercraft with it. In bed that night, Lenni put Rabbi Nachman away and turned to Randy. "He's worn the same clothes for days and he needs a shower."

"Please, just wash them when he goes to sleep. He needs to wear the same clothes."

The following morning Lenni put down a plate in front of Shane. On the table sat a frying pan, which earlier had been used to make French toast for the girls.

"I can't eat here," Shane said, standing by the table. Lenni didn't understand. The half banana on the plate was cut into five neat slices, how he liked it. The granola bar was unwrapped precisely an inch.

"That frying pan — it bugs me."

She picked it up wordlessly and carried it into the kitchen. What an odd duck.

Months went by before Shane allowed her an affectionate stroke to the top of his head. Once, while watching Lenni massage Julie's feet, Shane walked up and swayed from side to side, watching hungrily. "I'll do yours too," Lenni offered. He scooted backwards before she could touch him.

"I don't need for him to love me," Lenni told Randall as they brushed teeth before bed. "I'll just keep showing Shane love." It couldn't hurt to ask for his heart to soften a little. She fixed on Rabbi Nachman's words.

And may I enter into prayer.

May I express there everything in my heart.

Lenni brought Shane out to the uncultivated part of the garden. "You can grow anything you like here," she offered, pushing a shovel into the rich soil. "You like blueberries. Maybe some blueberry bushes?" Shane surveyed the area and scratched his head. He made a small "hmm" sound. "No, I'd get dirt under my fingernails."

A little boy who couldn't get dirty. He faded back into the house.

Lenni bought three blueberry bushes anyway and set the black plastic pots on the gravel walk next to Shane's designated area in the garden. After waiting a few days, she planted them herself.

Again and again she dreamed of her own little boy, furnace-toasty, crawling into the big bed with her and Randall in the morning. "Come snuggle," she would say, spooning her body around pudgy little legs, she and her baby drifting off to sleep.

◇◇◇◇◇◇◇◇◇◇◇◇◇◇◇◇◇◇

Lenni called the fertility clinic the week they paid off the legal fees. It had taken a year. Randall learned they needed to start with him—an immunobead test to prove nasty antibodies weren't hitchhiking on the tails of his sperm.

"Can't I just take in pictures of my son?" He grabbed his crotch in mock outrage, one hand on the steering wheel. They were driving in the van across Lake Washington to the Eastside clinic. "It works. It works."

It was kind of a date. Randall got to ejaculate. Then they drove west back across the bridge, Randy relating the details of procuring a sample for the clinic.

"Pretty weird," he said. "In the video, this woman comes walking along the beach with only a bikini bottom on and there are five guys sitting around and she says 'I'm horny.' Five guys. I kept wondering, is this film for women or for men, until I figured out they had five guys of different sizes and colors so that whoever you were, trying to jerk off, you could identify with one of them."

The clinic doctor required a perinatologist's seal of approval before he would set up Lenni's in vitro fertilization cycle.

The perinatologist was tan and courtly.

"I prefer to say advanced maternal age." Dr. Walker smiled, alighting from his white horse and pulling out a chair at the conference table. "Other terms can be so demeaning: maternal senescence, elderly gravida." He waved the phrases away with a flick of his Rolex-weighted wrist.

Lenni didn't care about the verbiage — one sounded like a refreshing herbal shampoo, the other like something that had been in the refrigerator too long. She just needed his approval.

Dr. Walker ran down the red-flag list. Regular periods, no toxemia with previous pregnancies, no gestational diabetes, no early labor.

"So why are you going IVF?" he asked, curiosity creeping into his polite manner.

"I was thirty-eight when my second daughter was born and thirty-nine — that seemed ancient even then — when my first husband left me. My new husband and I have been trying for two years," Lenni pleaded, followed silently with, *I want our own boy, a clean slate, not someone else's damaged goods.*

She saw the doctor's eyes drift over to her birth date on the form. He made no denigrating remark, the prince. Dr. Walker told her she was his first forty-six-year-old patient and declared her fit.

She wondered how her girls would take to a new baby in the house if she got pregnant. They had genially accepted Randall as the new man of the house. Yet, it would be another change in the family script.

Rachel, the thirteen-year-old, had washed her hands of Shane, calling him inscrutable, unsociable. Second daughter, Julie, two years younger, mostly watched. Her eyes followed Shane's patterns: how he wiped his mouth after each bite, where he crept to dismantle the alarm clock, how he stole matches and skewer sticks, how he never, ever wore a different pair of socks.

Shane started first grade. Each day after school, he quietly let himself in the front door and tiptoed up to his room, taking great care to close the door without a sound. From time to time, he emerged for rubber bands, paper or wine bottle corks Lenni saved. What, of mine, is he taking apart in there? Lenni wondered. The debris or a completed project often ended up on the dining room table by evening.

Once Shane was asleep, Lenni put everything back in his box and placed the collection outside his door. By bedtime the next night, gears, screws, and duct tape were all over the dining room table again. Lenni never said anything. She relished this unspoken dialogue.

As the school year continued, Shane began clumping down the stairs in the afternoons looking for Julie, who, with Rachel, attended middle school in a different neighborhood. Soon, he wanted to know exactly what time they were supposed to get home. Then, what time the bus let them off down the block. He emerged from his room earlier and earlier, pacing in the living room.

He asked once, twice, sometimes three times, "What time is it?"

Lenni checked the kitchen clock one afternoon. "4:10. Julie should be getting off the bus right about now."

Shane grabbed his jacket. He didn't remember to say he was leaving, didn't think to close the door. Lenni waited a moment before walking to the end of the driveway.

She peered around the hedge to the south. Shane's clumsy, nearly spastic way of running made him easy to spot. His unzipped jacket swung from side to side. His little arms worked the air in an anxious attempt to propel himself forward.

He loves Julie, Lenni realized, wonder-struck. He's opened his heart to her. She watched until she saw his tiny head stop bobbing. Rachel walked ahead with a classmate, followed by Julie, arms full of books and bags. Lenni imagined Shane wanted to hug Julie but did not know how. He would wait for Julie to put everything down and hug him, the space between them filling with something unformed, yet unmistakable in its effect.

To talk to the One to whom I belong.

"I don't get what you are doing that I'm not," Lenni said after dinner to Julie.

"It's not what I'm doing, really, it's who I'm not," Julie tossed back. "I'm not the evil stepmother." Lenni stared at the girl. Once she had jumped into her lap, now she was jumping on her heart.

"Not that you are," Julie hastened to say, seeing the sad downturn of her mother's mouth.

In October, Shane's school asked for a conference. Randall and Lenni sat across from a school nurse, Shane's teacher, and the district psychologist and heard the words "Asperger's Syndrome" for the first time.

"It's what makes him so different. Brilliant in some areas, socially inept in others," explained the psychologist, who wanted their consent to put Shane on small doses of Ritalin while in school. "We often see a family connection." Lenni thought of Crystal Waltham's inability to look directly at people, her muttering.

"He shows a spectrum of behaviors that could be classified as high-functioning autistic behaviors. Ritalin will help him focus better in the classroom."

They said yes.

Back in the fertility clinic for the injection lesson, Randall and Lenni watched the nurse demonstrate use of the syringes. The next morning Randall shook Lenni awake. He was teaching an early class this quarter and needed to leave. They stood in the chill blue light as he fumbled for the light switch and a syringe.

Lenni closed her eyes and tensed. In and out near her bellybutton, she felt the tiny needle shooting Dilute Lupron and Follistim into her system.

Randall tossed the syringe and relaxed. He was an academic after all, not a doctor. "Now I can tell you my dream. You and I were in the clinic with the doctors and the nurses and we were all dancing a hora."

Lenni laughed, suddenly lighthearted.

The daily injections created tiny pink pinpricks, which if drawn together in dot-to-dot style would have produced a squiggly smile across her abdomen.

Seven days later, an ultrasound showed that Lenni's ovaries were responding to stimulation. Her estrogen levels were appropriate. Days away from possible egg retrieval.

For that visit, Lenni told Randall to stay at work, a premonition perhaps. She would phone him with the results.

The clinic nurse moved the intracavity transducer up inside Lenni's vagina and adjacent to her ovaries. The follicles were not growing as they should, the nurse said. Only one was potentially harvestable, not nearly large enough. The doctor would not take a chance, at Lenni's age, on one chromosomally fragile egg.

Lenni tried to quiet her despair. "Knowing what you know, what would be your advice?" she asked the nurse.

"I can't see going forward with this."

Lenni and the nurse looked at the computer monitor and the listless numbers the transducer had registered. They did not look at each other. Lenni wondered if Randall should be part of this decision? It really had been her project from the beginning.

"We stop." Lenni sighed, unsuccessful in controlling her tears. The nurse turned away to clean the transducer. It seemed a long time before she turned back around, her nostrils a telltale pink.

"I'm sorry," the nurse said. "I'm about the same age as you. I never had kids. It's probably why I ended up in this field."

"Would you consider using a donor egg?" the nurse continued, turning the pages of Lenni's chart, looking everywhere except at Lenni. "I believe everything else is in your favor for an attempt with a donor egg."

"No." Lenni inhaled. Should she call Randall now or wait until she got home?

"I could end up raising somebody else's problems," Lenni murmured.

The nurse nodded and left the room.

Lenni reached for a tissue in the subdued light of the examination room. Disappointment hurts. Infertility hurts. Rejection hurts. Lenni was certain searing loss in suburban, twenty-first-century Bellevue, Washington felt no different than it did two hundred years ago to a Ukrainian man of faith upon hearing of his young son's death. She had memorized Rabbi Nachman's entire prayer.

She drove home, staring vacantly. Lake Washington's gray waters merged with the overcast skies. She wandered into the backyard and knelt down in her greenhouse. The ground was cold and bare. The tools, seed packets, and pots were stashed away. She picked absently at a weed. The kids were not home from school yet. Weary, she closed her eyes and lay down on the ungiving ground. Rabbi Nachman's words swirled through her brain.

And may all the foliage in the field
(all the grasses, trees and plants)
May they all awake at my coming

To send the powers of their life
Into the words of my prayer.

"Hey. I'm hungry. Will you make me some pasta?"

She rolled over. Shane stood in the greenhouse doorway. He seemed unsurprised that she was lying on the ground.

"I must have fallen asleep," she mumbled, getting to her knees, a little stiff, mouth sour.

She followed Shane into the kitchen.

"I'm a little sad right now," she ventured.

"Use the big pot," Shane said. "My father always uses the big pot."

"I could use a hug, Shane."

"Oh?"

"Well, I guess I'll just have to hug myself." Lenni wrapped her arms around her midriff. He stared and stayed put. She turned to the cupboard and pulled down the desired pot.

◇◇◇◇◇◇◇◇◇◇◇◇◇◇◇◇◇◇◇

Crisp fall turned into driving, chilly rain. One dark morning Lenni sensed a strange new weight in the big bed. Little feet curled around her calves like pea vine tendrils. Too small for Julie. She slowly registered the peculiar smell of boy. She opened her eyes wide. The discovery was hers to savor. Pillow over his head, Randall slept, unaware.

Had it been a nightmare? Had Shane woken up cold? Lenni looked over the small head to the slender volume on her night table. Next to the book lay her pile of crumpled papers on which she had written her responses to Rabbi Nachman's petition, a one-sided correspondence with a man dead these 200 years. Rabbi Nachman's final lines formed in her mind.

May my prayer and speech
Be made whole
Through the life and spirit of all growing things
Which are made as one
By their transcendent
Source.

She exhaled, long and slow, and listened to Shane's rhythmic breathing, a sound as numinous as any exalted words from a flawed world.

Gypsy Fool

My first boss used to warn me whenever my responses got too giddy, too flip: We Want Measured Tones, Classic Pearls of Wisdom.

I'd sneak in a few zingers anyway. The wilder my advice, the more letters I got. Bags of mail trump the most decorous and powerful editor, and, in my case, led to big-time syndication.

Now I let it rip. Dance naked in the sun. Steal onto your balcony in the dead of night and kiss your honey in the moonlight. Live large. Don't lose yourself. Never spy or eavesdrop. Know what you are running from. Don't base your happiness on the weatherman, at least in the Northwest.

Don't think for one minute the letters printed in my columns are made-up. My accordion files burst with thousands of letters — on parchment, on lined paper, on the backs of flyers, on file cards, even greeting cards — and those are the ones I keep. I get hundreds of emails a day. Some letters clearly are shot off after a heated argument. Some letters exalt the soul. Some break the heart. I've been answering people for a long time.

No one on Bainbridge Island knows I make my living as an advice columnist. I've learned I can't reveal myself or people will call and knock on my door day and night. Eventually, they would accuse me of playing God or shooting from the hip. It's why I moved to this isolated cottage. Even an advice columnist occasionally follows his own advice.

◇◇◇◇◇◇◇◇◇◇◇◇◇◇◇◇◇◇

After Grandmere's Tarot cards, my next best advisor is Bounder, my chocolate lab. In my opinion, wisdom is accumulated best through rubbing shoulders with another sentient being, preferably nonhuman. I watch Bounder scarf down his food and barf it back up, and I come up with a line, say, for impatient advice seekers to, "take small bites out of life and chew carefully."

Early mornings, Bounder and I do our chase-the-tennis-ball-in-frigid-Agate-Bay-waters routine. He thrashes through the wavelets as if it is the most important thing in the world to get that slimy green ball and drop it at my feet before winding up for a humongous spray fest with his body and tail. I gulp in the salty air and think, naively, that I won't get hosed this time. Right. I never jump out of the way fast enough. Hoo, it's cold! With both of us now wet, we run back to the house, where I towel Bounder off and leave my shoes outside before we go in for breakfast.

The dining room table — also my desk — sports an impressive array of used cups with small amounts of brackish liquids and stacks of mail. Once Bounder is finished eating, I let him back outside while I begin a bit of desktop archeology. Bounder loves to nose rocks and shells along the beach. This morning, his poking provides me with an image of people as stones or water. The stone people hunker down and take up a lot of room in the landscape; you have to navigate around them. The water people say things like, "Let me run this past you," or "You might consider this." Before you know it, a breathtakingly beautiful canyon has been carved out of an interaction you hadn't meant to let happen. Not to denigrate the rocks, but the land would be far less interesting without the two forms. I've been tricked into creating a few beautiful landforms.

I read through my first letter of the day. After a few deep breaths, I imagine the person who wrote it. Closing my eyes brings visions I prefer not to see, so I concentrate on Bounder, on the rhythmic wash of the waves, on the clever way day rolls into night and back into day. For truly vexing questions, I pull out Grandmere's cards from their now-tattered shoebox shrine and summon her spirit.

◇◇◇◇◇◇◇◇◇◇◇◇◇◇◇◇◇◇◇◇◇

Five gleaming swords on one card. To imagine owning such an arsenal sent my five-year-old self into paroxysms of throbbing thrill. I lobbed off the tops of my mother's flowers in the back yard, plunging my wooden approximation of a weapon deep into the innards of available bushes.

Grandmere called me over to the table where she sat outside with my mother. Her cards were laid out in what I knew was called a Celtic Cross, four cards at one end, another four wheeling around two overlaid in the middle. "Look who has come to pay us a call."

It was him; the beautiful knight with his impressive collection of steel. I wanted to kneel and surrender to this card. My fellow fighter. I would gladly fight to the death for him, lay down my life, anywhere, anytime.

"Five of Swords," my mother grunted, looking at the card, and then at me, worried.

My pudgy brown finger outlined the card, eliciting a cobra-like strike from Grandmere that left her fleshy underarms swinging.

"Don't touch," my mother snapped. "You'll only get hurt." Her warning stayed buried in me, like an oyster's bit of grit. Years of running and obfuscating coated that irritating tip for decades before it transformed into one of the Pearls of Wisdom hankered after by my editors.

My grandmother and mother must have known something was different about me. When I began to study Tarot as a teenager, I learned that the Five of Swords represents to act in one's own self-interest, to experience discord, to witness open dishonor. These are feelings very familiar to the Roma, even more so to a gay Gypsy.

◇◇◇◇◇◇◇◇◇◇◇◇◇◇◇◇◇◇

Dear Madame D,

I love my husband and I love my daughter, (my husband is not her father but has never questioned this.) My daughter's lesbian lifestyle has driven a huge wedge between them. How can I bring these two estranged people together before I die?

Della from Vancouver.

You're not going to bring them together. They will have to come together on their own. Feed them and hold their hands so that when you're gone, they can argue over your recipes and engage with the only other person on earth whose landscape has the same hole in it. I hope you were being dramatic about the dying bit.

Dear Madame D,

My partner, well, my girlfriend, well, we have three sons and a house, so we're like an old married couple, she reconnected with her high school boyfriend and she may be having an affair with him. He doesn't live in the Northwest, we do. I really need her to love me and the boys. I've put on some weight and I guess I snore like crazy, can't hear it myself, so some of the razzle-dazzle has dimmed. Should I propose marriage at this late date? I can't really talk to my friends or co-workers about this.

Darron in the Dumps.

Get thee to a gym. The rest will follow.

Dear Madame D,

How I comfort my teacher? Her baby so sick. My baby so healthy. Should I avoid subject?

Hopping yours truly, Lina.

Helping one life is like helping the world. Take your kids to a park and watch how intently they play. With the same intention, let your hands hold hers, and listen, listen, listen.

◇◇◇◇◇◇◇◇◇◇◇◇◇◇◇◇◇◇

Hidden by the dustups between my three older brothers and our parents, I got to observe — and exit — most family interactions at a distance. A final baby, our sister Antoinette, born a year after me, ensured that I would be left to my own devices. Fine by me. I spent most of my time in the company of my eternally patient mutt, Bebe, and my homemade swords and spears.

By age fourteen, I'd already lived on both sides of the Cascade Mountains: Federal Way, Chehalis, Centralia, Yakima and Othello. The used car business drew my father to the Seattle area, and it was there that Grandmere began teaching me Tarot, in secret. Several times a week, between customers, she and I sipped sweetened tea in her little shop, sandwiched between a gas station and a plumbing supply store on Highway 99 in north Seattle. She taught me that you learn as much from the customer as from the cards. Watch their faces, she'd say. Watch their hands as you turn over a card.

While it isn't forbidden for Gypsy men to read Tarot cards, they generally don't. It takes a certain amount of motivation. Let the women do it. It was easier for the men to cause a ruckus in one part of a department store while the women, elsewhere in the store, hurriedly stuffed perfumes and jewelry into their bags and down their shirts. I hated the sexist side of Gypsy culture. Why were the Gypsy men the peacocks and the Gypsy women only little brown hens? I was up against a code so rigid that to be gay was as much impossible as it was wrong. I would get physically ill when trips to the mall were planned. I would make money another way, I vowed.

A fellow ninth-grader, Cliff, had a paper route. He always had a pocketful of change and candy. Other routes were available, he told me one day after school, but he'd heard that Gypsies didn't like to work. Not this Gypsy, I responded hotly, sealing my fate with my tribe. Not only was I disinterested in girls, I got up very early and went to work. Clearly a *gajo*, a non-Gypsy.

About a year after I started my paper route, Grandmere was showing me cards in her shop when my father unexpectedly walked in. The Knight and, predictably, that Five of Swords had both turned up.

"Well, what should I know?" my father prodded. My grandmother, ever my advocate, swept up the cards. "They aren't talking to me today," she told my father brusquely. My father's ominous look made it clear he didn't believe her. My time was running out. I wanted to plan my departure before my father told me I had to go, before he ripped his clothes and called me *marime*, unclean.

Getting ready to be an outcast wasn't so bad. I did my newspaper route, went to school, hung out with Cliff, slept at his house many nights, and saved my money. I relished dawn's fresh newness, the solitary, sleeping kingdom of my paper route. I "found" a bike (some ways are hard to break.) I honed my aim, porch to porch. I bought a sleeping bag.

If I was to be an outcast, I decided to be a well-read one. My paper route had given me access to the world. When customers were on vacation or told me they would be gone a day or two, I kept their newspapers. I knew the names of all the reporters and editors — my imaginary family. Ann Landers and Abigail Van Buren became my aunties. I longed for my name to appear at the top of one of the articles or on the editorial page next to a serious-looking photograph. Carefully, I copied sentences and phrases I liked into a dog-eared notebook I lugged with me everywhere.

Antoinette and my mother kept me abreast of family news. They and Grandmere were the only ones who noticed my increasing absence. My brothers seemed indifferent. My father and uncles were barely polite.

I knew Antoinette's route home from school and bicycled by to talk with her now and then, which is how I learned one day that Grandmere was dead and my father was going to use her money to move the family to Memphis, where many Gypsy families lived.

"Can you meet Mom and me at home before we go?" Antoinette asked. Fearing a confrontation with my father or brothers, I told her to bring Mother to me.

Antoinette and my mother met me with a basket. We all cried, and my mother said she loved me and we would meet again someday, the cards had said so. Grandmere had wanted me to have her cards, my mother choked, handing me the old woman's mystically decorated shoebox.

I could have howled that night, so great was my sense of having been cut adrift. I continued sleeping at Cliff's house and, sometimes, in the newspaper shed. When he found out, Stephen, my route manager, let me live in his basement, where he and his buddies lifted weights. I started to work out with them, too, then just with Stephen. On my eighteenth birthday, he told me he had a very special present for me, and slid his fingers down my sweaty chest and into my shorts to show me what men can do for each other. From *gajo* to boy toy.

◇◇◇◇◇◇◇◇◇◇◇◇◇◇◇◇◇◇◇◇

Dear Madame D,

My grandson has gotten himself photographed practically nude on the cover of some trashy magazine. Don't think I haven't seen it. The old ladies who play Mah Jong with me all have grandchildren too and those grandchildren show their grandmothers such photos, especially when it is SOMEBODY ELSE'S grandson, and, thank goodness, not THEIR'S. My family thinks they can hide this but the truth will out. Should I confront my grandson and tell him he needs to change his lifestyle?

Oma in Tacoma.

Maybe he just couldn't find a thing to wear that day. There have been days when I've gone to my closet and, after endless searching, emerged empty-handed. This has never happened to you? Get the boy a gift certificate from some hip clothing store. I promise he'll put something on.

Dear Madame D,

I have a co-worker who lost his wife two years ago. He's been concentrating on keeping his two sons emotionally healthy during this time and has made no moves into the dating scene. Recently, he agreed to go out on a double date with my girlfriend and me and my steady guy— we are all in our late forties. Problem is, my co-worker and I spent the whole evening gabbing and having a great time. My co-worker and I are uneasy about what we may have discovered about EACH OTHER.

Rosie the Realtor.

No good deed goes unpunished. Or as my grandmother used to say, if you are going to kiss a thief, better count your teeth. Answer the following questions honestly and you will know what to do: What do I want from my co-worker? What do I want from my girlfriend? What do I want from my boyfriend? What do I want for me?

Dear Madame D,

In splitting up with my long-time girlfriend, I was informed that a viola she gave me wasn't hers to give. I'm about to embark on an extended concert tour with it and the last thing I want is bad viola karma. She won't reveal any details and I am left uneasy and unsure as to what I should do.

Restless in Rochester

Dear Restless,

Coax every heart breaking, soul stirring note out of your viola and let the Universe sort it out. As Plato wrote, "Music is its own moral law."

◇◇◇◇◇◇◇◇◇◇◇◇◇◇◇◇◇◇

A few months after Stephen and I became lovers, he got me a better-paying job as a manager on another route and helped me pay for writing classes at a community college. I started writing for the student newspaper while working routes for the big daily paper.

Nearly every day I smugly took inventory: lover, job, permanent address, easy access to drugs, parties, and writing instruction. Reinventing myself hadn't been so hard, I thought. I'd forgotten the first rule of Gypsy life—stay invisible.

After another great evening of pretty boys and alcohol, Stephen and I and a few remaining partygoers were chatting outside a downtown restaurant. The boys loved having their fortunes told. Most Gypsies won't read cards for friends—you find out more than you want to know about them. Not me, I liked the drama. Besides, it was a fun party trick and most illuminating for me. Grandmere's cards always told the truth.

A breeze made it difficult to light up my cigarette, so I moved away from Stephen and my friends and back into the sheltered entryway of the restaurant.

I took a long, satisfying pull.

"Can I bum a smoke?"

As if conjured up from the smoke of my cigarette, a brown leather jacket and a matching brown face loomed in front of me.

I handed over my pack and backed away.

The leather jacket came in close to my face. Was the guy coming on to me?

"*Romjah?*" Gypsy? He leaned towards me even more, as if to sniff, like a tracker dog.

"No," I said instinctually, and, by simply answering the question, gave myself away.

He looked me over coolly. "*Kasko san?* What tribe? I'm *Kalderosh.*" Russians, killers, potion makers, according to Grandmere.

"I'm *Machaja.*" There, I'd said it, breathing with difficulty. We were astrologers and lore-makers. Not psychics, however. Maybe this dude had been sent by my father or uncles to keep an eye on me — maybe to steal from or to hurt me. I shook my head. The alcohol and the late hour were making me paranoid; usually I'm better at assessing people.

The stranger slouched against the restaurant door. "You got people interested in your whereabouts, especially after I told them you knew Tarot and were doing it for all the fags here. Your name's Dario, right?"

I backed away, trembling, my breath coming in squeaks. Mr. Kalderosh left his hands in his pockets, emitting a whiff of menace, despite the benign smile.

"You can run," he said, almost grandfatherly. "You can't shake us. When we need to, we'll find you."

Grandmere's cards came out onto the table that night; they told me it was best to leave. In the mostly white Northwest, my olive skin and coffee-colored eyes were like beacons to other dark eyes. I wanted to be where I could blend in, where there was water and a shimmery sense of space, with a multiplicity of flesh tones. I panicked, and left for New Orleans, where I knew a few people and where the inhabitants — like the Gypsies — also loved sparkly things.

◇◇◇◇◇◇◇◇◇◇◇◇◇◇◇◇◇◇◇◇◇◇

Dear Madame D,

My husband flirts outrageously with any young thing. I feel it is so indecent of him — he is 75! I'm embarrassed to even be writing you. I don't like to go anywhere with him anymore but with our kids grown and no grandchildren yet, time hangs heavy on my hands.

Birdie the Empty Nester.

Chickens. Have him build a big run. You can care for and feed the darlings. And use a few eggs to throw at him when he is being really annoying.

Dear Madame D,

My mother died recently. In going through her papers—my father's in a nursing home—I discovered an apparent sexual indiscretion on her part. I don't believe my father or younger sister know. This discovery has been eating away at me. I am torn between telling my sister and letting this revelation die with me and my mother. My mother's correspondence with this young Black man is so beautiful and poetic. I understand a bit more about her and am haunted at what a prisoner of her time she was.

Dubious Daughter.

Go to a ribbon store. Luxuriate in the colors and textures. Find one ribbon you think your mother would have loved and tie up all her letters with it. Go outside and make a small fire with some fragrant pinecones and place your mother's letters into the fire. The priests in the Temple in Jerusalem were great proponents of deliverance through fire. You'll feel cleansed. Anything less would be voyeurism—unless you want to use the letters to write a steamy novel.

Dear Madame D,

I work for a garden company in their catalog division, accepting orders from people around the country. A couple of the girls and I in the phone order division realized that we get the same phone order from the same elderly woman once, sometimes even twice, a week. I've tried to dissuade her, which since I work on commission, is not in my best interests. I know the other girls just take her orders. Her credit card is good and my boss says we are simply following her wishes. What's the right thing to do?

Marigold Mary

Mary, Mary, on the contrary, maybe she wants to festoon the world with flowers. It's her secret tactic for helping people lead happy lives. Flowers give people something beautiful in their lives, something to take care of, something that cultivates connection. However, your concern is well placed. Next time you get her, ask if she has kids, get a name and phone number or contact her bank. They may have financial and/or co-signing information for you. A flower a day keeps the darkness at bay… a flower a day keeps us fresh and gay…

◇◇◇◇◇◇◇◇◇◇◇◇◇◇◇◇◇◇

New Orleans: a sensual overload in each sense of the meaning, even if I did have to carry two wallets—one with a few bucks for the hold-up guys, the other, hidden away, with the real stuff.

While writing for papers in the area, I spent the 80s and early 90s drinking, drugging, and rubbing up against some of the wildest bodies in the country. Then everyone started getting sick, and scared, and more careful. Committed relationships became the rage, and my boyfriend, Jerome, and I moved in together.

Before today's high-tech fertility clinics, same-sex couples who wanted kids could only borrow them, usually nieces and nephews. Jerome and I went around and around on the subject of kids for years until an exasperated female co-worker of mine handed me a turkey baster. Ask some of your doctor friends or put an ad in the newspaper for a surrogate, she suggested. For the right amount of money, you'll find a willing female.

We did find someone, though I can't legally reveal any details. My son, Spiro, and daughter, Aimee, were born, three years apart. I was never happier to shed my swinging past. Finally, I had stumbled into the heaven I desired. The kids completed me like nothing in my life had up until then (not even Jerome). Was it merely chance that the same week Jerome was diagnosed HIV positive, Aimee found Grandmere's dingy Tarot card box?

She came into the kitchen. "Dada, what are these?"

"Oh, my God, umm … aren't they pretty? How did you find them?"

Spiro joined us. "How do you play?"

I explained that the cards had belonged to their great-grandmother, and, in doing so, broke a spell. The kids realized Jerome and I were not the only ones in the world to whom they were related. Like the cards, the children were little mirrors to our reactions.

"Who is my grandmother?"

"She's probably not alive."

"Call her."

"I don't know where she is."

"You don't know where your mother is?"

"Do you have brothers or sisters?"

"I don't know where they are either."

"We could help you find them."

"You'll only get hurt." My mother jumped out of my mouth.

After the children were in bed, I placed the cards systematically in front of me, the first time in many years. Jerome was mesmerized. He had rarely seen me do this. He was full of questions. What does that one mean? Can you tell my fortune? How sick will I get?

Uneasiness crept into my heart at what I saw in the cards, and I brushed Jerome away. There must have been a reason Aimee had found the cards. Maybe a warning? I wiped the dusty deck and looked gravely at what lay in front of me: The Hanged Man, a symbol of letting go, reversal, sacrifice.

◇◇◇◇◇◇◇◇◇◇◇◇◇◇◇◇◇

Dear Madame D,

My son's been stolen from me by the court. The attorneys were so rude. Men are always rude to me. My ex and his conniving girlfriend haven't even bothered to get married. They throw their relationship in my face because I'm pretty much worthless. I have had a hard time being a good mother. Can you believe the forensic psychologist called ME hyper-vigilant? I'm financially independent thanks to my father's estate, but where's my dignity? I can barely get out of bed to feed my dachshund what with all the anti-depressants and sleeping pills I take.

Fairly fault-free in Ferndale.

Reflect on something you appreciate in yourself. In a brief brush with Buddhism, I learned that we contract and hide if we consider only our faults. Trust in your goodness and you'll be open to what's good in this world, and what's good in this world will open up to you. If you don't believe yourself, try seeing yourself through the eyes of someone by whom you've done right. I have a bumper sticker on my truck that says: "Lord, help me see myself the way my dog sees me."

Dear Madame D,

How can I deal with my overbearing, traditional Muslim family? I no longer wear a headscarf and I hate the way they treat us girls. When I try to discuss this with my brothers, they just shout at me and say I'm heading down a road of impurity.

Emancipated in Everett.

When Black slaves escaping the south saw women wearing Quaker bonnets, they knew the women would help them. What you wear does matter. How you behave matters more. Humanity is a giant ebb and flow of some people taking things off and some people putting things on. You take off your headscarf while some Orthodox Jewish girl gets married and shaves her head and puts on a wig. Make sure you are safe, educated and balanced. Can't hurt to invest in a sleeping bag in case a change of address is in order. Who you want to be matters the most.

Dear Madame D,

My partner of many years recently died. I am overwhelmed by this loss and by having to deal with the entrance on the scene of his estranged brother. My partner left his sizeable estate to me. I know I'd be taking the high road by providing something for the younger brother and that family's long-held farm, which is apparently on the verge of bankruptcy. My partner's family never disowned him, just ignored him. How much of a gentleman do I need to be?

Sorrowful in Seattle

Consider sending an amount to cover the farm's taxes directly to the tax man. Avoid handing cash to the recipient. An anonymous gift is the highest form of charity.

◇◇◇◇◇◇◇◇◇◇◇◇◇◇◇◇◇◇

Search. Separation. A long road. The Tarot cards kept turning up ominous displays, causing Jerome and I to watch the kids like hawks. Security consumed us. No play dates or errands went unchaperoned. Every minute was accounted for except the one, last August, at the crowded neighborhood wading pool where we spent nearly every summer afternoon. Spiro and Aimee, in a sea of clamoring children, had dashed up to a convoy of ice cream trucks, waving the dollars I had given them. Jerome and I, in animated conversation with friends, realized belatedly that the trucks had driven off and our children had not returned with ice cream bars.

Pursuit proved fruitless. A chase by police, friends, and us, produced only a bewildered teenaged ice cream truck driver. The poor kid couldn't stop trembling, terrified by the cops' attention and angry at the intrusion by strange, dark-skinned men into his territory. He had never seen the other drivers before, he said.

Jerome and I filed police reports and papered every town in Louisiana with posters of the kids. We emptied our bank accounts to come up with the reward money.

Each morning, half-asleep, I wondered why the children weren't up yet. Waking fully a moment later, I would writhe in bed from the oppressive silence of their absence. Creeped out that someone had been watching our movements, my body felt invaded, like eels were wriggling between my intestines and chest cavity. My skin and insides crawled with a vague remembrance of a brown leather jacket and an unsettling conversation decades ago. *Les yeux noirs*, the dark eyes of the Rom, had never been far away, after all.

I gave the detectives everything I knew about my family and the Gypsy community in the South and in the Northwest. Frantic as I was for Spiro and Aimee's return, in my heart of hearts, I also felt great resignation. My children had been reclaimed. Gypsies never forget their children or grandchildren. I had no status as a parent in the traditional Gypsy world. I was like a runaway wife or a divorce-seeking woman — even less so — in their sight. My people were simply taking back what they perceived to be rightfully theirs. The Gypsy people are few, every child counts; therefore, any Gypsy child in danger of being lost to the community needed to be saved.

My newspaper colleagues were uncomprehending moderns. Certainly, there always had been *stories* about Gypsies stealing children, they allowed, but that never really happened. I could not persuade them otherwise.

The Tarot cards were of no help nor hope, full of ambiguous juxtapositions and confusing configurations. It was as if the cards were torn between an allegiance to the Gypsy way of life and sympathy for my torment.

Jerome's symptoms got worse, and for me, life in New Orleans became sham and squalor. I sought solace, without success, in different faiths. By day, my advice columns gave me a reason to get up, barely. By night, even with sleeping pills, my dreams were so vivid that I woke up shouting and weeping: the children, shadowy eyes, Antoinette, and Tarot cards raining on our house like vengeful hailstones.

I began washing my clothes and hanging them around the rooms so I could hear them drip, drip, drip on the carpet — the sound of home. Not enough rain or dogs in my life.

Few couples survive the stress of a lost child. Or life-threatening disease. Or depression. Or tepid job performance. Or no job, as in Jerome's case. To have all of these curses heaped on us at once proved our undoing. I felt I couldn't save both Jerome and myself — *sauve qui peut* — save who you can. We visited an attorney, divided up what was left and got Jerome into an assisted living facility and on disability. Once our house sold, it took me only a few hours to pack my car and start driving back to the moist marvel of Western Washington. Grandmere's cards rode shotgun.

Madame D,

I read you every day and wonder who these crazy people is who write you. And here I is writing you about a girl with a well-meaning mother and no father to make her toe that line or let her know she is a valuable piece of work.

Old Auntie Coco knows how it is. A white woman mad at the Brother who got her pregnant and left. I'm still shaking my head over the man who walked out on me and my two boys nigh forty years ago, but I ain't mad. Mad makes you want to get back at him. Mad eats you up. Mad makes you eat. This woman's daughter, she mad. I tell her to sing them mad blues away. Oh can she sing. I tell her, Big Girl, if you can sing, you can love, and if you can love, you can be loved no matter your size.

Yours sincerely,

Coco

Dear Coco,

Size aside, we all have the ability to love big and be loved big.

Madame D

Dear Madame D,

My diminutive size has often been an issue in overcoming people's impressions that I am a lightweight in other parts of my life: relationships, leadership or musical ability. I'm a professional musician who stands on a stool to direct a choir! Sure, "good things come in small packages", but I've yet to meet a man who takes me seriously. They all treat me like a kid sister. My biological clock is gonging and I am longing. Do you have a Liszt of tactics?

VD

Dear VD,

Of all the art forms, I've heard that music takes the shortest route to the heart. If your life is music, look for someone who shares that passion—from the ivory-tower composer to the humble piano tuner. Surely someone within that range will think outside the Bachs and understand that there is the sound we hear in our ears and the sound we hear with our hearts. Being petite weighs small to the one who finds you and your musical stature desirable. Use Carmen sense. Non-musicians Offenbach at relationships with musicians because musicians are too Bizet gigging at night. Must close before I face the music from my editor and receive punitive measures.

Madame D

Dear Madame D,

I am writing this letter for a pashent. Now will come his words.

Dear Madame D,

My good friend Amina (that's me whose writing) often reads me your colums. I enjoy your witty and heartfelt responses but with all do respect, I want to ask you and your readers a question and supply an answer myself. Your readers strive for ways out of dilemas. You erge them to run after miracles, to try fresh aproachs, original paths.

Heres my question and my answer. Do you want to see something new? Take the same way home as you did yesterday. Talk to the same old people. Sit in the same seat in the 500-seat lecture hall. Lock your bike in the same bike rack. Then look around at the differences.

I traverse two 300-foot corridors every day, look in the same pashent rooms, out the same windows, into the eyes of the same aids. Everything the world is, everything the world believes in, has become part of me. You learn to see the same thing with new eyes. Before I became an invalid, I thought I had taken on the world, but now I know it took me somewhere too. I have learned that love doesn't stop when someone goes away or time passes or you live in different places. I have learned that sameness has its miraculous elements, that aceptance can be as true a transformation as change.

Peace,
Daniel Sinsheimer (and Amina)

◇◇◇◇◇◇◇◇◇◇◇◇◇◇◇◇◇◇◇◇

Everywhere I go, I look for Spiro and Aimee and I ask if any Gypsy families live in the area. Western Washington's Gypsies seem to have vanished. As the years drag past with no word of the children, I have gone from pain to some shred of understanding, from trial to trial until, looking back, the only sense I can make of this earthly journey is that we live on in the world in ways we cannot always know.

It has been a long time since my Five of Swords or my Knight has turned up. My card companions these days are more likely to be The Fool — faith and new beginnings — or The Hermit — acceptance and wise counsel, withdrawing from the world into a desired stillness.

I believe both fools and hermits collect stories. They even might write about sacred pilgrimages, be those paths happy or tortured, clear or half-remembered. Story weavers in each generation gather and preserve words and phrases for reuse or for return to a great, unseeable Repository. It would be unbearable to think otherwise.

My wrist watch beeps: 2 p.m., an hour before my deadline. I set aside some time to throw more tennis balls for Bounder. This gives me fresh eyes to come back and look over my responses before sending in my column.

I have never lost hope that one day in my bags of mail there will be a letter that reads, in Antoinette's familiar handwriting, "The children are safe. Someday you will see them again. It is in the cards."

Acknowledgments

With profound gratitude to my "village:"

June Anderson Almquist (1925-2000), columnist, reporter and editor, *Seattle Times*

Robin Asher, who grows books and gardens with equal mastery

Diana Brement, proofreader

Charles Gay, former editor, *The Shelton-Mason County Journal,* whose wordplay can be found in Madame D's answer to VD

Victoria Guy, She who triumphs over inanimate objects

Sandra Larkman Heindsmann, editor

Greg Herrington, former editor and editorial writer, *Vancouver Columbian*

Marti Kanna, copy editor

Brian Kohler, a designing spinner of yarns

Ruth Peizer, revered Yiddish teacher

Mark S. Radke, fire starter

Clay Sales, ice-dancing designer

Natasha Shtikel, Russian tutor and dear friend

Rabbis Beth and Jonathan Singer, who showed me holy is as holy does

Nat Sobel of Sobel Weber Associates, for his encouragement

Andrea Vahey, Gypsy guide

Shawn Weaver, forbearing partner and musical magician

and, of course, for *di kinderlakh*

About the Author

*A former reporter with the **Seattle Times**, **Vancouver Columbian**, and University of Washington **Daily**, Wendy Marcus co-founded, with Rabbi James Mirel, the Northwest's first Klezmer band — the beloved Mazeltones — in 1983. After a grand run of 16 years, the band gracefully gave way to numerous up-and-coming Klezmer ensembles and Marcus went on to build the music program at Temple Beth Am in Seattle's North End, where she serves as Music Director and editor of **Drash: Northwest Mosaic**, a literary journal.*